DREAMWEAVE

DREAMWEAVE

Mimi,
MAY YOUR DREAMS
BE FULL OF %0$AFL AA AA....

ERIK
GRAHAM

Nov 20/08

Mill City Press, Inc.

This is a work of fiction. Names, characters, places, and incidents either are the product of the author's imagination or are used fictitiously, and any resemblance to actual persons, living or dead, business establishments, events, or locales is entirely coincidental.

DREAMWEAVE

Mill City Press, Inc.
212 3rd Avenue North, Suite 570
Minneapolis, MN 55401
612.455.2294
www.millcitypublishing.com

ISBN - 1-934937-38-x
ISBN - 978-1-934937-38-9
LCCN -2008939095

Cover Design by Brent Meyers
Typeset by Sophi Chi

Printed in the United States of America

ACKNOWLEDGMENTS

Writing a novel is quite the undertaking. I would like to acknowledge the following, in no particular order, for their help and support while I acted like a nutcase getting this done:

To Brian Bradshaw, my old friend who when I explained about a bizarre dream I had that night about throwing a grenade out my window said, "No shit, I had a dream last night that I had a huge explosion out of my window!" I immediately made the comment, "Wow, imagine if they were interconnected? What a great idea for a novel!" Twelve years later here it is.

To Lisa Fox, my crazy partner in crime, who egged and egged me on to get it finished, and for all the support through thick and thin. Then, with many bottles of wine, helped me do the first serious edit and revisions of the first draft, and then the next....and the next....

To Scott Redman, my super tall friend that took on the task of typing out the first draft from all the various note pads and scribbles that made up the novel.

To Michele McMullen, my friend that sat with me for hours typing as I spewed out character and plot outlines.

To Pandora Siganakis, who did the first real professional edit of the novel.

To the Staff and Management of Joe Fortes Restaurant in Vancouver, BC, my local hangout where I spent many, many lunches writing and editing.

To Michele Shields, who did a fabulous final edit of this novel. What a difference.

To the 'Girls at the Cabin' who literally tore my manuscript apart so they could all read it one final time before publishing.

And to all the other people that I have talked to about this novel and the ideas, proof reading, encouragement and support they gave along the way.

Thank you all.

to my Mother Michele and Grandpapa Ti-lou
who gave me the writing gene

CHAPTER ONE

Looking out of the window of the New York City checker cab, Peter Sutherland couldn't help but notice the emerald colored sky above, but it did not register in his analytical mind. His gaze panned toward the driver who was behind a scuffed plastic barrier. Strange, Peter thought, the driver seemed familiar somehow, but he had never been to the Big Apple before. He settled back into the frayed leather seat and pulled out the dissertation he was to present at tonight's annual symposium. He had received the frantic call only two hours earlier back in Chicago. Two hours had not given him much time to research, theorize and write a dissertation on the comparative causes of quantum physics, all the while getting to New York by plane.

Peter looked back to the driver who was a large black male. With his curly hair coming out haphazardly from a beret too small for his head he said, "We're coming up on the hotel in ten minutes mister," with what sounded like a southern drawl.

"Thanks. What's a southern boy doing up in this stink hole?"

"Been here all my life, and don't knock my town unless you want to walk!" The driver shook his head and spit a large hocker out the window to emphasize his disgust.

Peter knew better to shut up, but that voice still came back and haunted him from his memories. Tokyo perhaps? No, he thought, but one hell of a coincidence.

Looking out again, he saw that the sky was now crimson red, but this still did not register up to his brain. His eyes drifted to the passing neighborhood, endless skyscrapers flew by. Ultra modern buildings mixed in with art deco smaller towers were fronted with countless sidewalks of teenage hookers and street people all trying to live another day. The city was a mess; litter and burnt cars were the norm, as it would be portrayed in a post-apocalyptic film. Peter felt a large, uncontrollable chill down his spine as the cab went further into the decaying borough, the blur of its inhabitants flying past the mesmerized gaze of the young scientist.

The cab slowed and pulled into a circular drive in front of a posh Six Star Hotel. A dignified and thorough uniformed doorman opened and greeted Peter with the efficiency acquired after many years of service.

"Please make your way to the entrance quickly sir," he said firmly. "We will take care of your luggage. Keep close to the guards please."

"Guards?" he said as he looked back toward the street. The surroundings had become more dangerous quickly, as a tactically outfitted squad of armed guards surrounded the entrance to the street and the hotel doorway. The same disheveled street people and now angry youth gangs taunted the guards. The guards stood at the their post motionless, seemingly oblivious of the masses. The strength of numbers and heavy weapons were deterrent enough. Peter briskly pushed the heavy revolving door into the hotel lobby and entered only to find an unreal calm.

Several groups of well-dressed patrons lounged on the authentic French Revolution furniture. The lobby was immense. As he looked toward the ceiling, he noticed a huge crystal chandelier hanging from the recessed circular focal point above. Craftsmen had spent months working on this room, he thought. His head turned back toward the street, but now all he could see was the expanse of black frosted glass. The huge lobby instantly appeared to shrink around him. He gave his head a shake and began walking toward the front desk.

"Peter Sutherland, checking in," he said, still in disbelief as he stepped up to the solid oak counter.

"Welcome to the Grand Manhattan Hotel, Mr. Sutherland. You have been pre-registered. Here are your key cards." The front desk clerk slid a small gold embossed envelope toward him. "Your bags will follow you to your room shortly. Please take time to familiarize yourself with the hotel security procedures posted in your room. Enjoy your stay," said the cute brunette, flashing that professional hospitality smile.

"What in God's name is happening out there?"

"It's been like this all over Manhattan for years, Mr. Sutherland. No need to worry, we have the best security money can buy," she said.

Peter thanked her and crossed over to the waiting elevator, pressing his floor number. As he waited, not even noticing the subtle music in the background he began thinking to himself. He knew that watching the news had not been a priority for the past few years, but had the country gone to hell without his knowledge? Plus, the damn cab driver was still familiar to him!

As he entered his room, the large suite pleasantly surprised him. "Glad I am not paying for this," he chuckled to himself. After taking a quick look around and grabbing an apple from the fruit basket adorning the central coffee table, he walked over to look at the view. Smog was everywhere, the city blanketed with what looked like an impenetrable fog that he had only seen worse in Mexico City. He could hardly see the tower across the street and he finally noticed the blasted frosted glass on the lower half of the window which made it impossible to see the street below. He started thinking about the street people but his eyelids started to sag, weary from the long trip. He went into the master bedroom not bothering to undress and lay down on the comforter, crashing as soon as his head hit the super plush pillow.

Opening his bloodshot eyes, he stared straight into the LCD of the alarm clock. It read 5:45 PM.

"Holy shit!" Peter said, and rolled out onto the floor. The presentation was scheduled for six o'clock, but luckily in the grand ballroom downstairs. Instinct took over as he ran into the washroom. He looked up to the hideous sight of creases in his face and messed up brown hair in the mirror. Splashing water on his face and running a comb through his hair, he started to try to get his mind on the lecture that he would have to present. Precious seconds passed, but he took the time to look again into the wall-sized mirror, pursing his lips as he noticed his wrinkled suit. He then gave himself the 'ol' Sutherland smirk and grabbed his briefcase and ran for the elevator.

"Peter, I thought you wouldn't make it," said a dapper looking executive. "Jesus, you look like shit buddy!"

"Sorry Frank, I overslept. When am I up?" Peter said excitedly, still combing his hair.

"You're up in one minute, now go stand over by the sound table," Frank said, pointing toward the front of the huge ballroom. It was filled to capacity, the air filled with excitement and a buzz of well-educated snippets of conversation. The brightest, and most recognized scientists in the northern hemisphere were there that evening only for one purpose, and that purpose all of a sudden had a huge lump in his throat. Peter made his way up to the front along the side of the ballroom, taking his notes out of his briefcase as he walked. The noise died down quickly as the sound of a well-practiced host took over the microphone. He nervously looked over the crowd, at the country's best, his peers.

"And now my fellow colleagues, it is my pleasure to welcome our keynote speaker of the evening, a young bright mind to the stage. One that everyone knows needs no introduction, Dr. Peter Sutherland!" a deep voice bellowed from the speakers. The crowd erupted into thunderous applause that snapped Peter back into reality. His shoulders back, he left the sound table and walked toward the stage steps. As he climbed the steps, the crowd's applause began to fade, first slowly, then to a deafening last clap. Walking along the front of the stage, Peter looked into the first rows of the elite, as everything else was blacked out by the stage lighting. Everyone was staring with mouths agape, looking like time had frozen.

"First of all, I would like to thank," were the only words Peter said before the entire room erupted into hysterical laughter. The distinguished delegates in the front seats were doubled over holding themselves, laughing so hard. The sound of laughter grew and grew to a high-pitched crescendo. The room began to spin as Peter's mind was whirling. What had he said? Did he really look that bad, he thought. The laughter only intensified, delegates now almost running out of the room to stop the pain from laughing so hard.

"OK, enough is enough," Peter yelled into the mike. "I can see that I will have to step off the stage!"

"You're," said a stunningly beautiful woman sitting in the front row, now almost hyperventilating. "NAKED!"

"What the Fuck!" Peter exclaimed as he looked down to his limp penis. The room started to spin uncontrollably. He staggered toward the steps to escape this madness. Tripping, Peter fell off the stage. The lights and sound dimmed as he headed into blackness.

Peter's arms flayed about, his hands tangled in wires, blinding light pierced into his brain when he opened his eyes.

"Hold on there, Pete-ol-buddy," a voice said coming from the surrounding brightness. A pair of hands was now working on the wires that Peter realized were attached to various parts of his body. He tried opening his eyes just a slit again. This time, trying to focus around the room. The room looked like your standard, antiseptic hospital room, the same as thousands across the country. A bank of monitors of various sizes and shapes took up the far left wall, dot matrix printers chattering off in the distance, and LED lights going on and off.

"Pete, will you PLEASE hold still while I take the rest of the sensors off. I swear to God, Peter Sutherland, I am going to put you into restraints the next time we do this. This is worse than untangling Christmas tree lights."

Peter stopped flailing around, and looked up at the voice. "Nice to see you too, Nancy," he said with a hint of sarcasm. He relaxed against the bedding, and studied her face. Still damn cute, he thought. It was good, no great, he thought again, that he had taken this young, twenty-five year old under his wing. The ironic thing was that Nancy Anderson was thinking the same thought as she kept untangling the wires; it was a good thing she had taken the job to save Peter's ass. Nancy was one of those girl next-door types: slim, slightly athletic with brown shoulder-length wavy hair. She was about 5'6", 115 pounds, had grown up in New York City and had the advantage of innocent looks, but with a street savvy about her. She was extremely intelligent, but didn't let on. She had worked her way through tech school to become a lab assistant and had had enough of New York near the end and decided on moving in with a cousin in Boston. She had found the job with Peter by answering a job posting on the University job board. Nancy found out later that Peter had a very small budget for his research facility and that this was not going to be a high paying job. However, she was intrigued by Peter's ideas on dreaming and his enthusiasm. She also thought it was really cute that he was nervous around her in the interview, so she decided to take the job and remain in Boston. However, her cousin had moved in with her boyfriend last month so Nancy now had the full weight of the rent. Luckily, she had some trust money her parents had left her, so the low salary was not an issue. She still had some breathing room.

She smirked as she took off the final sensor with more force than she had to. "You almost electrocuted yourself this time Peter," giving Peter a look that reminded him of his mother. He shook his head, as he had to get that thought out of his mind quickly.

"I'm just soaked! This is the third time for this. When did it start this time?" Peter wiped the sweat off his forehead.

"At three minutes into REM." REM stands for Random Eye Movement. Basically it's when your mind drifts off into a dream. Typically during a night of sleep a person will have several REM sleep periods where the most vivid dreams occur. "Your body temperature started rising to level off at 101 degrees at the six-minute mark. Peter, I am starting to get scared of this. How are we going to control this?"

"First, I want the computer printout of the body and brain sensors correlated to get the exact moment of the heat buildup," he said, swinging his legs out over the makeshift examination table. He was only in his boxers and was a bit self-conscious about it around Nancy. Hence the reason for the Bugs Bunny prints on the shorts to make him feel more comfortable. Secretly, Nancy thought Bugs was sexy for a rabbit as she looked at the shorts.

"Why now? What brought this on? Do you think we have gone into uncharted territory here?" Nancy asked handing him a plush towel.

Peter stood shivering, much to the amusement of Nancy. "Always the questions, hey Nance. If you weren't so damn smart and cute."

"Ya, ya, o.k. Let's get you into a shower and I'll start the analysis," she said and quickly turned around walking out of the room thinking of Bugs and blushing.

While Peter stood in the shower with the hot spray washing off the sweat from the experiment, he went through the latest dreams he had experienced the previous ten times at his small research facility. Peter had the ability to recall any of his previous dreams. Dreams were like movies to him. He had been like this since as long as he could remember. Others had photographic memory of anything they read. For Peter it was a visual record of his most bizarre alternate life - his dreaming life. He could recall any dream that he had had since childhood. Never two the same. Sometimes similar, but with differences that changed the outcome of his dreams. He had trained himself to make decisions in his own dreams. He actually could stop, think and deduct what was happening and sometimes alter the course of his dreams. Some would call that lucid dreaming but to Peter, it was just what he would do in the non-dreaming state of life so he didn't think of the process much anymore. He just lived out his dreams.

He was a bit concerned. His last three dreams, monitored at his facility with his own dream-tracking software, had been disturbing. He had not told Nancy that there had been more. He shrugged involuntarily in the shower as he finished lathering up. Nightmares. That is what he was calling them to himself, nightmares. They had been present also at night when he was at home in his own bed. Rarely did he get them, but now it seemed that they were prevalent in his psyche at this point in time. The most disturbing thing was that he, for the first time in years, was not able to control these dreams at the same level that he could his other dreams.

He stepped out of the shower and dried off with a worn out towel, slipped into his jeans and his favorite 'I Don't Work, I Just Dream' t-shirt that some colleagues had given him a couple of birthdays ago. He walked into his office off the lab room where he had just been strapped into and saw Nancy working at her work station with polysomnographic print outs all over her desk. These printouts, that Nancy called dream prints, were the graphic representation of REM sleep. They measured EEG, or electroencephalography, which measures the electrical activity of the brain or brainwaves. The dream prints also measured the time of rapid eye movement. With these two measurements, including the regular body monitoring, temperature, breathing rate and body movements that were being videotaped, they could try to pinpoint various points of the dream from Peter's recollection.

"This is the strongest of the three sessions according to the reading," she said not even looking up at Peter.

"Each session has become stronger," he said.

"Correct. What I'm concerned about is that, each time, your core temperature is getting higher. I don't know how much further we can go with this Peter. Your body can only take so much."

Peter did not say anything. He just nodded and thought, If only you knew, Nancy, that these are not the only nightmares that I have been getting. He didn't want to worry Nancy too much as he knew that she'd try to get him to stop this course of the experiments.

"Nancy, I am still in control of my dreams," only partially he thought quickly. "So until that point, we can continue. I almost made a connection this time," he said positively, "it was at the start of the dream, while I was in a cab, but couldn't get a hold of it. There was too much going on outside of the cab I was riding in, street people and hookers everywhere."

"Keep your wet dreams to yourself please," she said smirking as she kept looking at the data.

Peter blushed and cleared his throat, "I have a feeling that I am being drawn to these, well, I guess you could call them nightmares."

Nancy stopped and looked straight into his eyes. "Being drawn into? Do you get these at home?" she said with a look that he had seen before.

He gulped and his face flushed and said, "Yes, it has been happening for the last week." He looked away sheepishly.

She pursed her lips sternly, frowning while looking a bit to the side and confronted Peter as she said, "I knew it! Peter, do you not know that women can sense when men are holding something back? We are a team you and I. You have to tell me all your dreams, bad, good or even very good."

"Very good?" He now started blushing thinking of the last erotic dream he had had of Nancy.

"Yes, Peter. I want to hear about them."

Peter didn't answer again. He was trying to figure out how he was going to conceal that dream from her while he slowly buttoned his white lab coat to hide his now not so limp penis.

CHAPTER TWO

Situated on the top floor of the forty-story Zicon Corporation building in Manhattan, a meeting of the top three senior executives was in progress in the lavish office of the Chief Executive Officer.

"Ted, I can't believe what I'm reading in this report," Jack Montgomery, CEO for the last ten years exclaimed, throwing the thick report across his immense spotless desk. "Who came up with this garbage?" he said forcefully. This told Ted that Jack was not in the mood for smoke and mirrors. Jack had an energy about him that radiated authority. Standing 6'3" at the age of fifty-two with closely cut white hair, Jack had been the cover boy for many business-related magazines. He looked the part of the successful CEO billionaire. Zicon had been a small operation ten years prior, primarily surviving on existing patents from its Research and Development section. That is when Jack had stepped in and, smelling a bargain, bought the controlling share of Zicon. With his astute business sense and insider help, Zicon quickly became a very large player in the lucrative pharmaceutical and medical instruments industries.

What was not broadcast to the media was that Zicon was now a large multi-national conglomerate that had their hands into pretty much everything, including arms dealing, biological weapons and their antidotes, all hidden by shell companies multi-layered throughout the world. Zicon had just broken a sales barrier of one billion dollars in one year, making Jack a very wealthy man. Ninety percent of Zicon's pharmaceutical sales took place in South and Central America where regulations for testing and market placement were very relaxed. Silent board members were appointed from political officials' families in those businesses. Jack didn't mind getting his hands dirty. His thoughts were that money could fix any problem presented.

Jack shifted in his high backed leather chair. Subconsciously, he pushed up the sleeves of his Italian handmade engraved shirt revealing his excessive diamond clustered watch and stared right at Ted.

"Believe me Jack, I thought it was all crap myself until I had research take a look into it. Here's their report," Ted said handing it to him. Ted Jacobson, President of Zicon International, hoped that the report was accurate for his sake. Ted was Jack's right hand man, if there could ever be one. Jack's trust level was very low, but Ted maintained his subservient relationship with Jack, trying to find ideas to impress him and taking care of all the dirty work Jack cooked up. Ted was from Atlanta, Georgia, and had started at Zicon from the bottom as a telemarketer over twelve years ago, just before Jack took over. He basically bootlicked his way to the top, but was not happy with the result. He still had to grovel under Jack's constant onslaught. Now thirty-nine, and some would say bone thin for 5'11", Ted still had the weasel-looking demeanor that all the staff smirked about among themselves. Ted knew about the snide remarks and kept it to himself, cataloguing them in his head. He also headed Zicon's Corporate Security force, so he had ears everywhere. More like an industrial espionage and Delta force team, he controlled a small but very mobile and efficient army of agents trained to take on whatever tasks the CEO needed cleaned up.

"Christ, it's fifty pages long. Have you read this, Klaus?" Jack said as he looked over at Klaus Rowheidier, Vice President of Research and Development, European division. Klaus, now fifty and a bit over weight at 200 pounds and only 5'9", looked like an ageing professor with his full gray goatee. However, he was extremely bright, with an IQ in the genius range. He lived in Düsseldorf and tried to keep his work away from his circle of friends. Klaus, knowing how Jack was, kept his sarcastic humour in check for this meeting.

"I read my department's report on the flights from Düsseldorf this morning. I am amazed at the potential. Shall I summarize it for you?" he said in a thick German accent, which always reminded Jack of all the old WWII movies.

"I'm all ears," was the reply.

"First let me tell you that this is still in the research

stage. They started testing six months ago," Klaus stated.

"Who are they?" Jack questioned sarcastically.

"A small research team at the University of Boston. A young professor named Peter Sutherland heads it up. Dr. Sutherland started the project three years ago after being awarded his doctorate in Oneirology, the scientific study of dreams. He began his research as an assistant professor, intending to expand his thesis. Here is a copy that we obtained," Klaus slid across the desk another thick manila folder. Jack made a disgusted expression and waved in the air.

"I'll read this with the other one. Let's get to the reason for all of this. Something doctor, ah, what was his name?" he said trailing off at the end.

"Sutherland."

"Right, Sutherland. Where did he get this idea, or did he steal it from someone?" Jack stared across the table with a questioning look.

"According to his thesis, it came in a dream."

A look of disbelief came over Jack's face.

"It has been verified sir. Dr. Sutherland had been dreaming of driving through the countryside and stopped by a roadside cafe. The only other person in the cafe was another doctor. A Dr. William Olsen. They sat and talked for a few minutes and as Dr. Olsen got up to leave he scribbled a phone number on a napkin. Dr. Sutherland memorized it and after waking up, wrote it down. He then called that morning and reached... Yes, Dr. Olsen, who is a PhD in Communication Sciences at the University of

Copenhagen."

"Well, holy shit. Our people have talked to Dr. Olsen?" Jack said now laying both his palms on the perfectly pristine desk.

"I had CSU find him and interview him yesterday," said Ted. CSU stood for Corporate Surveillance Unit, better known by insiders as the Zicon army. Zicon had recruited the top disgruntled and underpaid tactical elite from North America and abroad. Large corporations were run like smaller governments and Jack's reasoning was that, as a small government, it better be armed, and so it was to the teeth.

"Any problems with his keeping quiet?" Jack said, raising an eyebrow.

"None. Dr. Olsen is quite happy," Ted answered quickly. Dr. Olsen had a propensity, Ted had found out, for flying to Asian countries to sample some of the young flesh for sale. CSU had merely obtained some very flattering pictures and video from sources that made a habit of filming all 'encounters' by foreigners to sell on the open market. Dr. Olsen was now happy about keeping very quiet.

"Good. Good work Ted. Go on, Klaus."

Ted smiled inwardly.

"Based on that dream, Dr. Sutherland," Klaus went on.

"Let's just call him Peter, OK?" Jack said now leaned back in his chair and looked out the window half listening to Klaus.

"Peter built the hypothesis that dreams by certain

17

individuals are intertwined with each other. For example, if I am dreaming that I am driving down a road in a car and someone passes me on a bike in that same dream, well then, somewhere in the world there is someone dreaming of biking and going past my car."

"Now wait a second," he paused, "You just said that certain individuals have this ability?" Jack said leaning across the desk, more interested in this conversation now.

"Peter has now expanded his theory that the whole world is interconnected, a sort of dream weave if you may."

"Dream weave? How does this work?"

"That is what Peter and his team are trying to find out. I have though, before coming here, done some extensive research and called in a few favors. It seems that this is not new thinking. Actually, it is over sixty years old and has been thoroughly tested. The basic theory is that all the dreams reside in a different dimension than our conscious bodies, outside of our bodies. Each dream would be independent of others, except when they collide. Kind of like two ships riding slightly different parallel paths that at some point would meet. When the two dreams converge, part of their dream would be in yours. Case in point, I had a dream last night of being in a large house and proceeded to open the front door. I was presented with a large ocean right at my doorstep. Why would that happen? According to the experiments of a very young brilliant German scientist during WWII, very disturbing experiments I might add, he concluded that the stronger dream could take over another's dream. He was able to become the stronger dream. In essence he could control the dreams of his subjects," Klaus said matter of fact.

Jack began tapping the fingers of his right hand on the table. Ted knew that tell very well. Jack's mind was plotting something, and it was not going to be pleasant.

"If we can get the key to this 'dreamweave', we could start influencing certain key players in our industries through dreams. Imagine being able to add thoughts and fears into the hearts of men who have no fear. Nobody could touch us," Jack said in a frightening tone.

"Exactly, Jack. Why do you think we brought this up to you?" Ted said supporting Jack's idea immediately while greasing the notion of his worth to the corporation.

"OK, Ted, you head CSU. Give me a status report and recommendations on how to proceed," Jack spun around and picked up his phone, completely indifferent that he now was totally ignoring the other two. Ted quickly looked at Klaus and nodded his head toward the door.

As they left his office, Jack did a turnaround and looked out toward the expanse of Central Park and smiled to himself. This was going to be a very good year, he thought.

As Ted closed Jack's door he walked side by side with Klaus down the quiet hallway to the area where Jack's executive assistants, all five of them, were located. Ted stopped halfway and turned to face Klaus.

"Where did you get that information on the German

scientist?" Ted asked almost in a threatening tone.

Klaus took a step backward to get out of Ted's space and replied sarcastically, "I am the head of Research and Development you know. We do know how to find out information the old fashion way by asking around, not by using the Gestapo tactics that your so called CSU agents seem to relish."

"Listen, you son of a bitch," Ted was now using a very low but forceful voice as he poked Klaus with one finger in his chest, "I want to know where you got that information and from whom. I also want a full dossier on what you know about this German and his present whereabouts."

Klaus was now fuming inside. His thoughts ranged from little piss ant ass-licker to wanting to wipe that smug look right off Ted's face with a good punch. He hated working for Zicon since Jack had taken over, as he was also one of the old guard like Ted, but he had seen Ted rise through the ranks and knew he would be trouble. For five years he had put up with these two egomaniacs and their illegal practices! He had seen and heard many disturbing things and although he wanted to leave so many times, he was always pressured. No, he thought, let's call it what it really was - threatened to stay as he knew too much of what was going on. What Jack and Ted did not know about was the expanding file of information that Klaus had on the 'dirty' enterprises that Zicon conducted in the Third World unregulated and unsupervised countries. He could bring down Zicon with one phone call and that gave him the strength right then to place a sly smirk on his face that infuriated Ted even more.

"Well of course, Herr Jacobson," he said smartly as he did a bit of a movement upward on his toes and clicked his heels together just like a German officer.

This enraged Ted even more. His face went red, and just as he was about to let loose, Klaus spun around on his heels and walked over to the executive assistants leaving Ted with his mouth open just ready to speak. As he passed one of the assistants in plain view of Ted, he stopped, took out a thin manila envelope and handed it to the now confused assistant.

"Could you please have this delivered to Ted Jacobson as I am catching a plane back to Germany right now," he said with an air of joyfulness. He didn't even wait for a reply and turned and walked out the door without another word. The assistant looked down the hallway to Ted with the folder in her hand and an embarrassed look on her face. Ted just stomped over and snatched it from her. The assistant looked away immediately and went back to work. The rest of the assistants stopped talking and all made themselves busy. Ted walked over to a side conference room while trying to open the manila folder. His breathing was labored as he was still fuming. Almost getting a paper cut from his shaking hands, he finally got it open and took out three sheets of paper.

The first paper was a brief bio on the German scientist, a Dr. Fritz Rhinefalt. Ted read onto the next page and his flushed appearance suddenly turned deathly pale.

CHAPTER THREE

Many miles south of the town of Jaco on the southwestern Pacific Coast of Costa Rica, a weathered-faced, white-haired, very spry German man shuffled along. The well traveled path went from a secluded small house surrounded by palm trees on a hill overlooking the ocean. The small path, once chocked with ferns, lead down a smaller cliff to the private beach and pier with a twenty-foot open motor boat. The early morning trek was routine after twenty-five years. He enjoyed the solitude of walking on the volcanic black sandy beach with no one in sight. He was completely secluded here since his beach ended in huge rocks on each end. This had become his sanctuary. Sanctuary from his sins. Rounding the last bend on the path back to his little cabaña, he heard voices. His sanctuary was over. They had found him. He walked with the same gait, no fear in his posture. What was there to fear for a demon like himself?

He hadn't started out as a demon, but had been transformed into one from childhood. Born into a long line of medical professionals in 1921, he was influenced by his father who was an expert in pharmaceuticals and chemicals. From an early age, his father recognized that the family gene for genius ran strong in his boy Fritz. So, from the young age of seven, his father had him not only watch but also participate in his experiments. Experiments of a hideous nature testing new drugs and chemicals being funded by the old regime of Germany, waiting for the next war to come. Fritz was fascinated by the results of his father's concoctions. He was oblivious to the sounds of suffering and agony from the caged animals at his father's lab in the small town of Zistorsdorf, near Vienna. By the age of ten, Fritz was conducting his own experiments, much to the pleasure of his father. By twelve, he was already well on his way to becoming a master chemist, but he needed a more stringent education in medicine. So on his thirteenth birthday, his father enrolled Fritz into the medical school at the University of Vienna. Small for his age and also being extremely young, it was not easy for Fritz. However, he focused on his studies and became enamored with one of the professors who lectured about the emerging trend in neural-networks of the brain. He became fascinated with learning how chemicals could and would be able to fix any and all brain-related ailments. During his third year at the age of sixteen, Fritz, while listening to another lecture half-heartedly, heard the words 'mind control' from the speaker. Immediately his mind went into a frenzy of new ways to use his knowledge, completely ignoring the rest of the lecture or the blonde fraulein that was trying to get his attention. The next two years passed quickly for the now brilliant man, no longer a boy. He had obtained his degree in medicine at seventeen and joined his father for a brief time mixing inhumane concoctions for the building Nazi war machine under the new Führer Adolf Hitler. Every spare moment was spent on his new theories and experiments. Controlling the minds of others was all that he thought and talked about. He had prepared, over a few months, certain drugs that needed testing and verification - verification with live human subjects. His new Nazi friends were happy to accommodate him.

"Dr. Rhinefalt?" A well-dressed CSU agent asked, standing at the entrance of the pathway to the beach.

"Herr Rhinefalt," the old man said, without emotion.

"Herr Rhinefalt, we wish to have some words with you."

"I think the arrangement will be that you will talk, I will listen. Am I correct?"

"Herr Rhinefalt, we have not come to harm or seek atonement for your actions. On the contrary, we are here to protect you and ask for your cooperation," the agent smiled, the sun glinting off his mirrored sunglasses.

"I am still listening," he said as he had no other choice. The pathway was filled with the bulk of this man.

"I represent a powerful group of men that have taken a keen interest in your field of study."

"My field of study has been ostracized."

"On the contrary, Herr Rhinefalt, your field of study is well and alive, although not to the degree of your esteemed self," said the CSU officer looking at the doctor with an admiring look.

"I did not detach myself from the scientific community for the last thirty years to be patronized Herr...?"

"Cantaloga. No disrespect intended; quite the opposite. My superiors have read your journals and assumptions. They wish for you to continue your work." The agent shifted his feet.

"Continue my work and be labeled worse than the Barber of Seville?" he said still standing motionless.

"Continue your work and be heralded as the father of a new awareness," the agent raised his hands to the sky.

"Ahh...so you are familiar with my projects?" Dr. Rhinefalt said inquisitively.

"Only in the most general terms. I am to be your liaison. Your gopher, if you may. You ask, I get," he said taking off the glasses and looking directly into the doctor's gaze.

"Research facilities? Staff?"

"Only the best money can obtain. Anywhere you want it located," the officer smiled to himself knowing that the doctor was now on board.

"I have become accustomed here. It is very quiet and the local officials are deaf mutes for a price." The doctor took a look over the shoulder of the agent toward his property.

"We can start by you giving me a list of facilities and equipment within 24 hours. All will be arranged. Your property here actually will be easy to setup and secure. Time is of the essence."

"You mentioned my research being alive and well?" the doctor now shuffled past the agent, wanting information. His body might have been old, not as old as many at that age, but his mind was still a steel trap. He was already formulating his requirements and making lists of procedures that had been left undone or would be tried again, this time with modern equipment.

"Yes Herr Rhinefalt, a small team headed by a Dr. Peter Sutherland is currently conducting dreaming experiments in Boston. I have brought you the latest information and reports that we could obtain." The agent was now following the 5'6" wiry frame toward the house at the edge of a two-acre grassed area surrounded by thick palm trees and tropical foliage. Yes, very secluded, he thought.

As Dr. Fritz Rhinefalt opened the door for the agent, he stated, "So, it is a race. Who will cross over first? Let us make some coffee and start this list."

CHAPTER FOUR

"Tony? Tony? It's Peter in Boston," the words were muffled and digitalized since the call was traveling a long distance.

Tony replied, "I've been waiting for your call old buddy."

"What do you mean waiting?"

Tony smiled to himself and thought of the first time they had met. It had not been quite three years ago in Tokyo. Something had compelled Tony to go to one of his favorite restaurants called Bakaratei that night. It was a warm and cozy local place that served traditional Japanese food. He had enjoyed his meal, talking once in awhile with the owner. While he sipped his after-dinner drink, he noticed a Caucasian man enter the restaurant. Must be lost, Tony thought, looking around the room toward the all Asian clientele except for himself. The owners sat the lost sheep at a table nearby. Tony looked at the man. The man looked average. Average height, not overweight. Looked American, not European but there was something there. Tony could sense a connection with this man. Part of his being told him to speak.

"You look like you speak English," the American man spoke. Startled, and embarrassed Tony realized he was staring at the man.

"Ah yes, yes I do," Tony replied in a deep voice, clearing his throat midway through his answer.

"Great, you wouldn't happen to know what Shika Penisu is?" Peter said looking up from the confusing menu.

"Yes, I do and I know you don't want that," Tony instinctively lifted his glass and rose out of his seat, crossing the floor to the man's table. "Tony Blake," he stated, extending his hand.

"Peter Sutherland," as he applied a firm gripped pump of the hand. "Sit down, please. Texas?" he asked nonchalantly and shifted some of the items on the table to make room for his new friend.

"How did you guess?" Tony chuckled.

"Well, sometimes it is the luck of the Irish," said Peter in an over pronounced southern US drawl.

A hearty laugh erupted from Tony. His deep sounding southern accent in Tokyo was well known, as was his 6'5", 250 pound frame that hovered over the population daily. The tables around them began to return to their meals, gossiping between themselves over the brash Americans nearby.

"This is not the usual dining fare for a fair-skinned American," Tony surmised, taking a sip of his drink.

"I flew in this afternoon and started wandering around.

I passed by this place twice. Each time I had a chill sensation. I live in Boston. I like chills," he said placing his menu back down on the table.

"So Peter from Boston, are you really hungry?" Tony said with a smirk.

"Not at all. Still five in the morning for me right now," he said and by habit looked at his father's old watch he treasured.

"How about a drink then? I know of a spot down the street," Tony said, getting up from the table.

Ordering their drinks from the Oriental cowboy attired waitress, Peter flinched as a high note was cracked by the karaoke singing Japanese businessman. Peter looked around the vivid colored room almost in shock mostly from being thrown into a completely strange environment. The place was busy. The purple velvet benches and stools were all full with well-dressed businessman smoking like it was the last day on earth.

"Have a couple of scotch, and you will be singing along," Tony quipped.

"You seem to know this place... I mean Tokyo, well," Peter questioned.

"Have been here for twelve years or so. It grows on you," Tony smiled.

"My first time. I decided I needed something different to see. Used to the same old in America. Tokyo kind of stuck out there for some reason. You play ball in the States?" Peter said looking at the huge man, changing the subject to find out more about Tony.

"UCLA. I got a football scholarship, but never got into the jock mentality. Guess riding my loud motorcycle around campus was not the in thing," Tony chuckled.

"Scholarship huh? An educated biker then. Nuclear engineering?" Peter said sarcastically.

"Actually, medical engineering - brain stem stimulus recognition," Tony said speaking matter of fact.

"Wow, that's a mouthful. Funny thing is that I just read up on that a couple months ago after having a dream," Peter said enthusiastically.

The cowgirl was back with the drinks. Nice six-shooter's, Peter thought as she sauntered away.

"Tell me about this dream," Tony asked sipping his scotch and looking over the crowd but keeping Peter in the corner of his eye.

"Ok.... strange though. I am sitting in a university classroom in the dream. I look up at the clock and it's 3:30. I look around and the class is listening to the professor. I look down toward the professor who has a fresh brain in his hands. He is talking about stimulus impulses into the brain stem. I seem to know what he is talking about," Peter took a second sip of his ten-dollar beer.

Tony smirked as he finished Peter's sentence. "Then a girl from the class asks the professor about a diagram on the chalkboard behind him. The professor turns around to face the board. Then I notice the hole in the professor's head where his brain should be,"

"Whoa, how in the hell did you know that?" Peter

shouted, his voice not noticeable by others because it was drowned out by the music.

"I was there also my friend," Tony said, shaking his head. "I was sitting in that class too."

It had only taken a millisecond to remember those thoughts of the past, but Tony felt as if it was yesterday.

"I am flying out to Boston tonight Peter, we have to talk... talk in person."

CHAPTER FIVE

Such a nice morning, Manuel thought as he peddled his bike. The morning trip was a daily ritual for the fifty seven year old Costa Rican farmer. Dressed in slacks and a button-down short-sleeved shirt and a wrap-around brimmed hat, Manuel looked like he was heading to church. Actually, he was headed for his weekend game of chess with his old friend Luis. Manuel had been playing chess with Luis since he was a kid. Growing up in rural Costa Rica near the town of Parritta, he had not ventured further than two hundred miles in his whole life. Well maybe only once, going to San Jose, the capital, for a wedding. His parents, both history buffs and teachers, had entertained their children with stories of legends of the past. Stories of ancient times, where powers extended beyond the physical boundaries of earth. Luis enjoyed these recalled stories while playing many rounds of the masters' game with Manuel. After, they would tend the teak tree plantation they had both built over the last fifteen years. Life was good and relaxed as he bicycled along the path to his next chess match.

He took a right after the town of Parritta and headed

toward the Pacific Ocean. Luis lived in a modest house along the single road on the Isle of Palo Seco, a mere half a mile away over a very short one-lane bridge. They were actually going to play at the local bar called Mari Sol on the island, with its open-air thatched roof patio overlooking the ocean.

What a beautiful day for a game, he thought. The road narrowed before the small bridge as the dense brush tried to reclaim it. He moved over to the right as he heard a vehicle coming up behind him. Luis was bound to lose his luck today, he thought, three games he had won in a row. It was his weekend. He could taste it as he saw the bar down the road while coming up to the bridge.

The vehicle slowed as it pulled up beside him. "Hey, you speak English?" asked a pretty blond from the car. Manuel stopped his bike at the passenger window.

"Si, a little," he replied.

"Which way to Jaco?" she asked him with big bright eyes.

He looked passed the woman and glanced at the driver, a preoccupied looking man. Manuel turned his head, looked back and pointed, "You all have gone the wrong way. You will have to…" Manuel fell to the ground convulsing as 50,000 volts from a stun gun pulsed through his body. Manuel's streak of bad luck had carried on.

"Hey Boy!" Luis yelled in Spanish from his seat in the Mari Sol bar cornered on the main island road. Everybody went by this bar. The boy slowed to a stop and answered back, "What do you want?"

"Where did you get that bike?" Luis knew Manuel's old piece of shit bike anywhere.

The boy became defensive, "It is mine."

Luis calmed himself, as he didn't want the boy to ride away, "It is ok, I know this bike. It is the bike of my friend Manuel. I've seen this bike for longer than you have been born."

The boy was scared but stayed put, "I found it. It is now mine," still trying to show some backbone.

"Where? Where did you find this bike?" Now Luis was really curious and getting worried.

The boy gulped and pointed behind him, "On the other side of the bridge in the bushes."

"How long ago?" Luis looked at his watch; Manuel should have just been arriving.

"About ten minutes ago, there was no one around the bike. It was thrown away," the boy said still trying to justify himself.

"You saw no one on the road?" Luis now got up and looked down toward the bridge.

"No one," he paused, "except the car that almost hit me. It was driving very fast."

"Which way was it headed?" Luis's alarm bells went off in his head.

"Back toward the main road to Parritta."

Luis knew that something was wrong. Manuel never missed a game. Never. Also, no one local drove fast on that road. It was too narrow. "Boy, you can keep the bike,"

Luis said as he approached the boy, "but I want to know everything you can remember about that car and who was in it."

Manuel woke up groggily. The silence was complete. He opened his eyes slowly, the lids still very heavy. Utter blackness. His heart raced, where was he? Or was he dead. He tried to cry out, but only a muffled effort reached his ears. It reached his ears, he thought. Well, at least that was something. He started concentrating on feeling anything, pain, touch, anything. His fingertips touched something cold, probably metal he surmised.

White heat blazed in his head before he closed his eyes.

"He is awake then," Fritz commented to one of his new assistants. He had just turned on the lights. For the first time in years, Fritz felt alive again, his research reborn. Over half a century had passed since his first experiments.

CHAPTER SIX

The summer of 1943 saw the German war machine in full swing. Fear, with names like Auschwitz, brought horror to millions. At one of the lesser-known concentration camps, Janowska in Poland, a young twenty-two year old German scientist who was also a SS Hauptsturmführer Officer was experimenting in advanced forms of mind control and manipulation with the use of drugs and pain.

The subject before him was strapped down to a table, stripped naked. The subject was in extreme agony, writhing, straining to be free from the bonds. His eyes were wild. No recognition of the present, only pain. This went on for another twenty minutes. Fritz just stared at him, observing, occasionally writing down a note. The subject stopped writhing, shuddered and died.

"We are getting closer!" Fritz exclaimed. "Another four or five tests and we should have the right dosage ratio."

"What time frame are you looking at?" asked the lower ranked SS Untersturmführer Officer.

"One week. One week and I will be able to start stage two of the project," was his reply.

"This is good. The High Command is looking for a favorable report this time," smirked the officer.

"I will require another five subjects - strong ones. And I need to get the ratio right before starting on the POWs."

"I will send them over immediately," he saluted and left the office.

The new subjects arrived that afternoon. The look of defiance was still in their eyes. They have not been to the main camps, Fritz thought to himself. Perfect, still a fight in them.

Jacob stood with the others, his face and scalp freshly shaven. Dressed in camp clothing, he wondered how he had escaped the madness of the camps. Was this place any better? He was taken to a small sterile room and told to undress. Then he was placed in restraints in a large wooden chair. He looked around the pristine room with white ceramic walls. The same ceramic floors graded slightly to a drain in the center. Easily washed, he thought for some reason. He was left there until midnight with the lights fully on.

"We shall start administrating the drug now, since they have all been prepared," Fritz commanded his assistants. "We shall use a lower dosage first and increase it hourly," he carried on, "I want them all alive this time."

The experimental drug had been developed over the last two years. Its final purpose was to manipulate a subject's mind and let the manipulator add memories, suggestions or a command that later could be activated. In a sense, a walking time bomb.

Jacob realized that he had been awake now for over seventy-two hours. After they had injected him, the hallucinations began. More from the lack of sleep, the mind wandered from reality to the subconscious. His eyes could not stay open. Waves flowed through his body. Waves of comforting sleep signals. His mind and body near the breaking point of exhaustion. They had kept him awake all this time, moving him, taunting him and examining him.

First, his mind shut down completely. All but the basic functions became inert. His body relaxed, the muscles finally released from their tension. An assistant came in fifteen minutes later to check on his reaction to the drug. Alarmed to see the subject slumped over in the chair, he rushed over checking for a pulse. Many had died at this stage. Allergic reactions had been the cause of most deaths.

"A pulse," stated the assistant happily. Fear filled his mind as Dr. Rhinefalt had demanded, no, had threatened, that all the subjects must be kept awake so that the controlling suggestions could be tested and evaluated. The assistant in fear of his job or life, tried to wake Jacob up. He shook, slapped and doused him with water. Nothing made Jacob stir.

"Why is this subject not awake?" Fritz screamed from the doorway. The assistant turned around to see Fritz's red-faced and crazed looking expression.

The assistant stammered out an answer, "He was like this when I did the fifteen-minute check up. I can't wake him up," he took a deep breath. "He is not responding at all."

Fritz, still red-faced crossed the room. He also checked for a pulse and then checked the leads attached to Jacob that were wired to the monitoring device, a machine designed by Fritz to read the neural electrical activity of a subject.

"Get some smelling salts," he demanded. The assistant ran down the hall frantically searching. Fritz started mumbling to himself, "This is not good, what am I going to do with these subjects. They are not reacting properly." He shook his head and anger built up within him. "God damn them," he burst out loudly; he knocked over a tray of implements that crashed to the floor. "I will send them all to the camps!"

The monitoring device started up, the needles registering electrical activity from Jacob, and Fritz's mind went into a frenzy once again looking at the readings.

He hung upside down, completely disoriented. The smells were overpowering. His hands free, he tried undoing the restraints on his chest. Locked. What was he doing here, Jacob thought. He looked around at a room with no doors or windows. What was that smell? He looked down and saw his own feces lying below him. He realized he was completely naked, attached upside down on a wire rack. He started to fight the restraints.

"Be still and listen to my voice."

Jacob looked around; no one was in the room. The sound was all around, but from no specific point.

"You are part of an experiment. The temperature in the room will increase. We are going to slowly increase the temperature to a maximum of 200° Celsius within the next half an hour. All we require is your physical reactions to the change."

The room temperature started to rise immediately. Jacob again pulled at his restraints as the panic gripped his mind. As the temperature rose, sweat started running into his eyes. The metal restraints conducted the heat well and began burning his skin. Within the first ten minutes, the temperature had risen to 65°. The air was turning very heated. Every breath was painful. The screaming started at 120°. His flesh felt as if it was on fire, turning bright pink. The restraints were now searing the exposed flesh. At 150° the screams had turned to strangled moans of agony as Jacob's tongue had increased to twice it's size. His flesh was now a bubbling mass supported by bones. Jacob ceased to be at 160°. Twenty-five minutes into the experiment, his body had cooked itself.

Fritz looked down at the remains of Jacob. He and the assistant stared in disbelief at the body. The skin had turned black and blistered. The smell was unbelievable.

Jacob was still restrained in the chair. The chair had no indication of heat exposure. The restraints looked exactly the same as they were thirty minutes ago.

The camp Kommandant walked into the room moments later and said, "Herr Doctor, a report has just hit my desk stating that you will have results within one week. I wanted to verify this before informing the High Command." The Kommandant took his eyes off of Fritz and followed the assistant's gaze to the charred mass on the chair. "What is the meaning of this Herr Doctor?" he asked.

"Your results Kommandant," Fritz said straightening his back. The assistant quickly looked at Fritz with shock. "I moved to the next stage of the testing today."

"Then why the report of one week for results?" The Kommandant said sternly.

"Never show all your cards, Herr Kommandant. I was to let you know in two days what happened here today. You could then report before the week was out. You and I would be looked at favorably by the High Command."

A grin came across the Kommandant's face. A very young but wise doctor, he thought. "OK, please explain to me what happened to this," he said pointing at Jacob.

"I have been experimenting on mind control through the intake of drugs. Many drugs or multiple combinations of drugs have been used. The object of the experiment was to be able to control a subject by drug-induced mind control. It had not been successful until now."

"To be frank Herr Doctor, looking at your test subject, it does not look successful to me," said the Kommandant looking at the still smoldering Jacob.

"On the contrary Sir. I injected this patient earlier today and then, when the patient fell asleep, I tried the next phase of the experiment. Dream manipulation."

Again, the assistant looked at the doctor with alarm. What was he saying, he thought.

The Kommandant scoffed, "Dream manipulation?"

"Yes, dream manipulation. I am now able to control a subject's dream patterns and make them dream what I want."

"So again Doctor, what happened to this subject?" Fritz could tell that the Kommandant was getting impatient.

"I told the subject that he was in a room, hanging from a metal rack, and that the temperature of the room was going to rise to 200° in half an hour. This is the result, he cooked himself to death."

"You expect me to not only believe this, but to also report this to the High Command?" the Kommandant yelled.

"Kommandant, I will set up another test for you to observe. This should calm your skepticism," Fritz said, giving the Kommandant a competent look.

"Set it up today," he commanded.

"I will have everything ready within two hours," Fritz said with conviction.

The Kommandant took a long hard look at Fritz and then left the room without a word.

Fritz turned around to face the assistant, "Find me a subject that is exhausted and sleeping if you can. Turn off the lights to the cells. I need them asleep."

"Sir, we cannot report this to the High Command," he said shakingly.

Fritz's face turned red again, "There is no we! You will do what I ask. The experiments will go on, and the High

Command will be informed. There'll be no mention of how this came about. Do you understand?"

The assistant just nodded. He knew better than to push his luck, "I will find you the subject, Herr Doctor."

The assistant looked into the examination rooms of the remaining four subjects. One was in and out of consciousness and the subject in the next room was sleeping. Notifying Fritz, the assistant injected both subjects at the same time, in case one did not respond.

The Kommandant arrived two hours later, skeptical to view the experiments.

"We have administered the drug to this sleeping subject half an hour ago. You will notice that he is restrained in a similar chair as the last subject," Fritz informed him.

"Yes, yes, I can see this doctor, let us begin," the Kommandant said impatiently.

Fritz simply nodded and began speaking to the subject through a microphone, "You are in a room with no windows. You are hanging upside down. You can see your environment. You are held by metal restraints on a metal rack. You are naked. Look around the room."

The subject started moving his head around as if he was looking, but with his eyes closed. "Why am I here?" he asked.

Fritz smiled, "You are part of an experiment. The temperature in the room will increase. We are going to slowly increase the temperature to 200° within the next half hour. All we require is your physical reactions to the temperature change."

The subject immediately started trying to get out of his restraints. He was jerking around in the chair with a look of horror on his face.

"Hold still, or we will increase the temperature more rapidly."

The subject relaxed a bit, but started whimpering. Within ten minutes, the subject started jerking around trying to get out of the restraints. Sweat was pouring down his face. The Kommandant just kept staring. At eighteen minutes, the subject was screaming and convulsing. His skin was turning red and blistering. Blood spilled out of his mouth as the subject screamed.

The Kommandant could not believe what he was seeing. What a weapon, he thought. The subject died four minutes later, almost tearing himself from the restraints, ending in a blood-curdling scream.

Fritz was about to say something to the Kommandant when another scream erupted. They quickly looked back, but the subject was clearly dead, his swollen tongue hanging out from the side of his mouth. The screaming continued, but sounded muffled. The assistant rushed in the room all flustered. "Sir, come quickly to the next room," he said.

They all ran to the adjoining room and viewed a similar scene. A subject in the final throes of death was burning up in his restraining chair. Seconds later he also died. Both the Kommandant and Fritz looked at each other. Fritz had a small smile on his face.

CHAPTER SEVEN

Peter was there to pick Tony up at the Boston Airport.

"This is twice now that you and I have been in the same dream," Tony said hurriedly, while getting into Peter's SUV.

"True Tony, but you didn't have to come halfway across the planet to let me know that." Peter said as he gunned the engine down the arrivals' ramp and headed into the thick traffic.

As they started toward the University, Tony explained, "You have mentioned your theories on dreaming being interweaved. We have both had experiences with this."

"Right, and now I am trying to re-create this in a clinical study," Peter sighed.

"It has already been done," Tony dropped the bombshell.

Luckily, Peter had his concentration on the road as he took a quick look at Tony, "What? Do you have proof of this?"

"I mentioned your theories to a couple of colleagues and I received a report two days ago from Germany from an undisclosed sender. Inside it was a report by the U.S. Army back in 1944. The report was of dream experimentation by a German doctor at one of the concentration camps. The report is a bit vague, but it was claimed by a captured assistant scientist that drug-induced subjects were used as guinea pigs by a Doctor Fritz Rhinefalt for a year of dream experiments. The assistant claimed that they had been successful in inducing nightmares in subjects in separate rooms, each having the same nightmare while in a dream state. Most of the subjects died during the experiments."

"This is incredible! I can't believe that I did not hear about this before," Peter said as he shook his head and lowered the volume on the radio.

"The report, classified as top secret was never verified. The assistant, who was to be questioned more in-depth, died in his sleep a week later," Tony coughed, "The report was set aside, probably as a hoax. There were other things to find in that camp."

Peter said nothing for a few moments, his driving now in automatic mode, "Amazing, dream experimentation since 1943 using nightmares. I would never have thought of or even contemplated that. My God, it must've been hideous." Peter's eyes had a glazed look about them.

They arrived at the University and entered Peter's research lab, just as Nancy was getting off the phone. She waved at them and said, "OK, thanks for the info," and hung up.

"Nancy, this is Tony. Tony, the world renowned

Nancy," Peter said, with force.

Tony chuckled, and like a true Southern gentleman came over and kissed her outstretched hand, "My pleasure, ma'am."

Nancy smiled at the comment, nice looking too, she thought. "That was Jill in records calling," she turned speaking seriously to Peter, "she said that there have been inquiries about our research."

"From who?" Peter said cautiously.

"She didn't know, but was going to try and find out," Nancy said as she was sizing up Tony from the corner of her eye.

Peter looked over at Tony with a something's up look, "This means we're on the right track. We are making someone either nervous or curious."

"And with this information about German war experimentation, I think I'll be staying for a while," Tony said, grabbing a chair and facing more toward Nancy.

"I appreciate that Tony. We can use the help and expertise," he said.

"German experimentation?" Nancy jumped in. Tony went on to explain what information he had been given. A look of shock came across her face. "Wow! What a discovery. Know any Germans?" she said kiddingly.

"Actually, come to think about it I do. Klaus Rowheidier. Ran into him at a symposium a few years back. Haven't talked to him in a couple, though." Nancy noticed that Tony was staring at her computer. "Let me see if I can find him."

Nancy got up from behind her desk and waved Tony in, "This is all yours, sir."

Tony smirked. Cute and sassy...hmmm, he thought.

The morning was not going well for Klaus. Two assistants off sick with the flu and progress on the new Ebola vaccine had hit a brick wall. He also had to get the monthly report ready for video presentation by tomorrow. A dozen calls had rang through to his office and it was only 11:00 A.M. Time for coffee, he thought as he got up from his desk. The phone rang. Automatically he picked up the line without checking the caller display.

"Klaus Rowheidier, Zicon Pharmaceuticals," he said robot like.

"Klaus, this is Dr. Tony Blake, we met at the International Symposium on Computer-Based Medical Systems in Prague a few years back," he said in a friendly tone.

"Tony Blake? The Texan, correct?" Klaus said, squinting his eyes.

"Yes, big black Texan. I'm calling as I have received a World War II report addressed from Germany last week, with no reply address. You are the only German I know," Tony said leadingly.

"Tony, I am sorry, but your search is not done. I never sent you a report. Not to be rude, but I was stepping away to a meeting. Do you have an e-mail address? We should catch up on events," Klaus said hurriedly.

"Ahh, sure Doc," Tony gave him his e-mail address

and said goodbye. "Well, that was strange," as he said putting down the phone. An inquisitive look came across Tony's face.

"Knew who you were?" Peter asked.

"Yes, but I know the brush off when I hear it," Tony contemplated, looking down at the phone.

"Europeans are a strange bunch," Nancy quipped in. Peter and Tony both looked at her humorously. Nancy shrugged, "I've dated a few."

CHAPTER EIGHT

Ted got out of his limousine on the corporate airport tarmac and headed toward the Zicon seven seat private jet. He stopped in his tracks as his pocket started vibrating. Whipping out his sleek satellite phone, he waited a second and then said into the receiver, "Secure."

"Sir, this is the CSU European section head. We may have a breach with a department head named Klaus Rowheidier. Text as follows, in transcript."

The SAT phone's video screen became a text page with a phone conversation transcript. It took ten seconds to read. "I agree," he replied, "find this mentioned report discreetly in his home. Locate any other related material and only copy. Leave them undisturbed."

"I'll report back in twenty four hours," replied the agent and the line went dead.

Ted boarded the luxurious seven-seat jet, and told the captain to start the departure. He hit a speed dial number on his SAT phone as he sat down on one of the supple leather seats. The whine of the twin turbofan engines began, but was muffled by the soundproofed fuselage. The

SAT phone dialed out. "Ivan, communications," came out of the speaker very casually.

"Ivan, this is Ted. I need some of your magic. Copies and continual tracking of e-mails for a Dr. Tony Blake and Dr. Klaus Rowheidier. Also send out an sniffer for dream experimentation reports, Germany, World War II."

What Ted had asked was Ivan's specialty. Former teenage computer hacker who was responsible for breaking into the British SAS database, Ivan had been recruited by Zicon after his brief jail term for their industrial espionage needs. A so-called 'communications' specialist, Ivan was in his element now at Zicon. Deep inside Zicon headquarters, protected by a vast array of counter intelligence and eavesdropping veils, he was in his own cocoon of digital bliss. Surrounded by a dozen computers all tied to a super computer mainframe and an Internet connection pipeline that would make a small government envious, he would be called a Uber hacker in some circles. He could touch almost anything he wished that was connected to the Internet. Because of his talents, Ted overlooked Ivan's state of disorder, dreadlocks and grunge clothing. He looked like he should be living out on the street.

"Can do Boss," Ivan replied, "Notification?" he asked.

"Just myself for now," Ted said. "Super quiet, OK?"

"I think you are losing your confidence in me," Ivan stated sarcastically.

"OK, OK, I need it in twenty-four," Ted hung up, shaking his head. One of the best recruits he had ever acquired. Ivan had never even noticed that Ted had hung up on him, as he was savagely attacking his computer keyboard. Calling up prewritten hacker scripts, Ivan modified one he had designed for searching and capturing e-mails residing on Internet service provider servers. The scripts shot out into the cyberspace of the Internet searching for e-mail tags inside of header codes. Headers on e-mail messages had the pertinent information of from whom and to whom the e-mail was sent and received. It first searched for Klaus's multiple e-mail addresses which were known to Ivan, even the secret ones. Once found, the script went through the thousands of e-mails that Klaus had sent or received looking for a mention of Tony Blake.

It found one that was five years old, where Klaus had sent a thank you message to Tony for dinner at the symposium that both had attended. It now had Tony's email address. With this new information, it then searched the Internet for all e-mails that Tony had ever received or sent out. Within minutes, copies of e-mails sent to and from both e-mail addresses started filling up a new directory on his computer. While this was happening, Ivan wrote another type of sniffer script that would search throughout the Internet, far more accurately than any search engine, for the term that Ted had asked for. Hitting the enter button, Ivan sat back and took a long swallow from his triple sugared cola. Drink of choice for some hackers.

He turned around to turn up the volume on a jazz tune playing on one of the many computers still humming around him. Turning back to his main computer he saw that an indicator was flashing showing that a data file had been found from his sniffer script. The file came from deep within the U.S. Army archives, but his script had hacked right in and grabbed it. Double clicking the file, Ivan opened a text file and started reading. Three minutes had passed and he never even noticed the jazz tune had ended. He sat there with an expression of horror and amazement on his face.

CHAPTER NINE

An hour into the flight, Ted's SAT phone chirped. A text message appeared on the handset telling him to access his private mailbox on the company's Intranet, a secure network similar to the world wide Internet but strictly for Zicon's employees and officers. Opening his laptop he logged into his mailbox and opened an encrypted file left for him. The file opened and filled his screen. The document was still unreadable, just a bunch of mixed characters in no legible pattern. Ted opened a de-encryption program written by Ivan. It prompted him to enter a ten-character password. After entering the password, the file started to appear.

The heading of the file was 'Top Secret Report on Experimentation at Janowska, Poland, 1944'. It went on with a brief description of an experiment with dream manipulation. The rest of the file started to appear line by line. Ted got up and made himself a drink while the file materialized. Sipping his gin and tonic, he sat back down and looked at the screen. His drink slipped from his hand and landed softly on the plush carpeting. His eyes were riveted on a black and white photo of the charred remains of a human form strapped to a chair. He quickly scrolled down to the next photo and saw a similar scene. A third photo showed a room with four of the same strapped to chairs all in a row. You could read the agony of death in their faces. To the right side of the last photo, two German officers stood with their backs to the camera. The profile of one was recognizable, a young Fritz Rhinefalt.

All of a sudden the magnitude of the project hit him. It was as if they were dealing with black magic. The question was, was it controllable? Ted sat back and closed his eyes dreading the rest of his trip.

The jet landed in San Jose, the capital of Costa Rica, in mid-morning. The humid air of the tropics filled the cabin as the door opened. A jet helicopter was waiting for Ted. He got onboard with Mr. Cantaloga, his head CSU agent for the area.

The helicopter lifted off the tarmac and headed west toward the Pacific Coast, one hour away.

"When was the last time you were out there?" Ted said into his headset microphone.

The agent heard Ted through his headphones, as the engine noise was extremely loud.

"Two weeks ago. We were asked to round up three subjects for the Doctor to start live experiments. We delivered the subjects to him and he then requested to be left alone. Of course I told him that this could not be done, as we would have to guard the place. All we have there is a small team of five agents securing the compound. I did not want to antagonize the Doctor, so this will be the first visit since the experiments. I did inform him that we would be visiting him today."

Ted, now knowing the full extent of the tests, was worried about inquiries of the missing subjects. "Where did you acquire the subjects?"

"Our first was taken from a remote side road far from the research site. The other two were found squatting on property fifty miles from here. They will not be missed."

"Will the first one be missed?" Ted yelled, still trying to be heard over the rotors.

"It was a clean capture. No traces," the agent replied looking out over the lush jungle terrain, not knowing about the bike being left behind.

"But will he be missed? Was he also a squatter as you call them?" Ted sounded impatient.

"No, he did not seem like a squatter, his clothing was clean and neat," the agent said as he began to worry.

"I want this perfectly clear, find out through your channels whether anyone reported him missing. We do not want a witch-hunt here. Understand? I also want security doubled at this site from today on. I don't care if he wants to be left alone. We cannot afford to have this compound breached. Do you understand?"

"Yes sir," Cantaloga gulped. He then began making arrangements for the rest of the trip.

The quick flight came to a close when the pilot

announced they were approaching the compound. Ted asked the pilot to do a circle around the compound before landing. The helicopter started a banked left turn heading out toward the beach. Ted leaned against the window, the centrifugal force pressing him against the wall, and took his first look at the compound below. The whole property was over five acres in size. They were now skirting the east side of the property. It was lined with thick jungle foliage that ran from one end straight down the beach. The compound was on a thirty-foot embankment that sloped sharply to a black volcanic sand beach. Huge rocks blocked any entrance to the beach from the east, starting at the bluffs, they continued jutting out into the ocean. An S-shaped path descended from the clearing at the top down to the beach, with a smaller path jutting out from one of the turns, leading back into the east jungle. The helicopter was now over the ocean swinging back toward the property. The same rock formation blocked off the western approach to the beach.

What a find, Ted thought.

Like the eastern edge of the property, the western edge was a wall of thick jungle foliage. A modest one-level beach house was perched overlooking the beach on top of the embankment. The helicopter flew over the closely cut grass of a huge lawn toward the main two-story house and a recently built equipment shed. It finally completed its circle, flying over two large army-engineered structures housing Fritz's research lab, the compound security control booth and the barracks. The roofs of both buildings teemed with satellite and microwave antennas. Heading back down the east side, the helicopter slowed and hovered over a freshly paved helicopter pad, fifty feet from the entrance of the path to the beach.

Cantaloga opened the helicopter door and lowered the ramp. The white-haired doctor came out of the research building with a burly Tico, a Costa Rican native, dressed in hospital whites following close behind.

"You must be Dr. Rhinefalt," Ted extended his hand to the old man and introduced himself. "I am Ted Jacobson, President of Zicon." Fritz remained silent as he also put out his hand. Maintaining the hand shake, he stared intently into Ted's eyes.

The uncomfortable silence was broken seconds later as Fritz replied, "Thank you for coming to see the results of your research dollars, Mr. Jacobson." He released Ted's hand. "I like to size up a man that I do business with by looking into his soul. I want to be sure that the person behind the money can take the responsibility and burden of what he is purchasing."

Ted stared at Fritz. Fritz turned and started walking toward the research building. "Let me show you what you have purchased," Fritz said with his back to Ted. An uncontrollable shiver went down Ted's back as he followed the old shuffling man, knowing he would only find horror.

CHAPTER TEN

Klaus walked out of his apartment building's elevator and started down the narrow hallway. As he reached his apartment his neighbor's door opened and an elderly petite woman, immaculately dressed, stepped out to start her daily affairs.

"Herr Rowheidier," she said with a surprisingly strong voice, "Good morning to you. Working late again?" she asked.

"Yes, Frau Bäcker," he said not turning around. Such a nosy bitch, he thought. He placed his key in the door lock, fumbling a bit trying to ignore her.

"Where did you find a carpet cleaning company to work throughout the night?" she said as she locked her door.

Klaus froze. "It was not easy," he said controlling the tremble in his voice. He turned the lock.

"Did you see what time they finished?" he asked knowing that of course she would know. She would know their eye color if he asked her.

59

"They left an hour ago. You can tell them that even though they tried to be quiet, I heard furniture moving all night," she started down the hallway. "Please inform me next time you plan to do this again," she said with a scowl, entering the elevator.

Klaus opened his door, stepped inside and quickly locked it. With his back pressed to the door, he listened for a full minute before moving. His mind was whirling with thoughts, knowing exactly who had been here. He had requested from CSU a similar act years ago on a suspected employee.

He started walking through his apartment. Nothing looked out place. Ghosts left more evidence than these professionals, he thought. He opened his liquor cabinet and poured himself a double 14 yr single malt scotch and took a long swallow. A sinking feeling hit his stomach as he nodded to himself. The call from Tony. He had to assume that they had bugs on his phones, probably on everyone's phone. Goddamn Zicon, they don't trust anyone, no matter how high up, he fumed to himself.

His analytical mind kicked in, the panic was over.

So, he thought, they know about the call, which means that they know about an old report from WWII. They do not have this report as it is still hidden. And I can't check on it, as they will be following me.

His mind began its analytical assessment. He took another sip of his scotch. He knew that from now on everything he did would be monitored. He immediately walked over and turned on his stereo to a classical radio station. This was normally what he did when coming home. While the violins played in the background, Klaus planned his next move. His moves to outsmart the sly fox he worked for.

CHAPTER ELEVEN

Vincent had been restless all night. Business was going well, almost too well. His latest venture was growing too quickly. His cash flow could not match the growth. He tossed around on his king size bed inside his luxury condo in downtown Manila. The young man from the Philippines just wanted to get some sleep, but with sleep came his recurring dream of the last few nights. More like nightmares, he thought. He had taken a sleeping pill a half hour earlier and it finally started kicking in.

As the relaxing action of the pill took hold, his mind finally calmed for the first time today. Fifteen minutes later, Vincent entered into Rapid Eye Movement, the beginning of the dreaming sequence.

The cerebral cortex is one of the main centers of the brain for dreaming. Sensory experiences are fabricated by the cortex as a means of interpreting a stream of signals from the brain stem.

As the stream grew stronger, images appeared - random images of past experiences and dreams. Then within a nano-second he was within his dream. His dream was not within him. The energy charge of his dream, his dreamline, shot out from his cortex into an undiscovered dimension - the dreamweave. Vincent's dreamline shot into the dreamweave at the speed of light, traveling in a straight linear line.

Within his dreamline, Vincent was in a desert trying to escape the heat. It seemed like he had been walking for days. His clothes were in tatters, his lips cracked from the relentless sun.

His brilliantly bright dreamline continued on into the endless black dreamweave dimension. Another dreamline approached Vincent's line at a slight angle. It continued closer until it glanced off Vincent's line, but not before it had joined his line for the briefest of moments.

Vincent kept stumbling along the top of dunes. He stopped and looked out at the vast emptiness of the desert. Dunes as far as he could see. Despair engulfed once again. Then, from over the top of a dune in front of him, a bearded man in a top hat and tails rode a nineteenth-century bicycle toward Vincent. Vincent stared at the large front-wheeled vehicle as it went whizzing past him. The gentleman riding high above him tipped his hat as he went by, the tails on the suit flapping in the wind. The bike and rider carried on over the endless dunes effortlessly and vanished within seconds. Vincent looked out over the desert once again and continued his trek, the sun getting hotter still.

Vincent's dreamline continued on, but now took a slightly different course since it had been touched by the dreamline of the bicycle rider. Minute's later Vincent's line then came close to another dreamline that started running parallel to his. Both lines had incredible energy from the dreams being generated within. The other dreamline was still slightly stronger than Vincent's, so eventually the two lines crossed and joined for a moment.

Vincent walked over another dune and then tripped onto asphalt. He cursed as he had scraped his palms and knees on the gritty surface. He quickly got up as the heat of the asphalt burnt through his pants. You could see the heat radiating from the pavement. Vincent looked around and was completely disoriented as the desert had disappeared. He now saw only pavement. He noticed what looked like a structure far away. He started toward it. Walking for what seemed like hours, he finally saw a huge concrete building painted with strange symbols. It was stark against the paved landscape.

A scene out of a 'B' rated sci-fi movie transpired next. A large open-air military vehicle with no wheels, hovering over the ground, went by him. It was filled with uniformed men carrying strange weapons and awkward doglike clothed creatures.

Vincent's dreamline disengaged from the other dreamline.

Vincent was again in the desert alone, falling down into the choking sand.

The other dreamline intersected Vincent's dreamline once again and he found himself on the floor of a high walled concrete cell staring into the eyes of the doglike creatures. Three of them started to surround him. One began an unearthly growl and rose up onto his hind legs, approaching Vincent. Vincent backed toward the wall in complete terror. The creature gnashed his jaws and lunged at Vincent. Vincent jumped to the floor and landed on top of a dune and tumbled down toward the bottom of the never-ending sand.

The other dreamline had disengaged and went on its separate way, its course altered by the interaction. But this temporary connection had altered Vincent's dreamline course also. His dreamline traveled on passing other dreamlines. If one could ride on top of a dreamline, the sight would be one of the most beautiful visions imaginable. Bright laser like lines shooting through darkness. Silver beams of light crossing constantly, touching and making small flashes. A myriad of dreamlines making a complex weave through the dimension, almost like billions of miniscule shooting stars traveling through space.

In the path of Vincent's dreamline a growing mass appeared. It was comprised of a dozen or more dreamlines trapped and interweaved in a spiral formation - a dreamhub. The dreamlines had been caught almost like gravity to the energy being generated by several other dreamlines. The linear path of the dreamlines coming close was interrupted and as more of them converged, the dreamhub's energy increased and attracted more dreamlines. The spiral grew in a counter-clockwise rotation, similar to what a black hole might look like. Inside the trapped dreamlines, the stronger or predominant dreamlines took control, projecting out images and energy. The dreamlines that were now part of the hub were influenced by the overall positive or negative energy that emitted from the dreamhub.

By the time Vincent's dreamline approached the dreamhub, it was made up of hundreds of lines. Spiraling faster and contracting within itself. Vincent's dreamline joined the hundreds of dreamlines spiraling in a counter-clockwise, contracting negative dreamhub.

Vincent's despair was now unequaled. It felt like he had been walking on these dunes for days, with no nightfall. The insistent sun beating on him. Then, out of nowhere, a sudden energy wave went through him and his surroundings. A rolling distortion wave projected outward and then sharpened behind it. He followed the progression of the wave as it grew. It reached the horizon and continued upward into the sky toward the sun.

Vincent continued onward and then turned toward the sun, noticing that it was changing color into a hue of orange. The air around him was also changing, becoming super dry as the temperature started to rise. The sand became hotter underneath his boots. Seconds later, he found it painful to move his arms through the heated air. High above, the sun was now turning crimson.

The temperature climbed and the air soon became an inferno, his boot heels melting into the sand. He clawed at the buttons on his shirt as they seared his skin. His flesh bubbled in spots and flames started flaring all over his body. His agony immeasurable, he looked up for what he knew would be the final time to the source of his anguish, the unforgiving sun. The now almost blood-red orb contracted against itself and exploded into a brilliant super nova.

Vincent saw the flash and his last smile of relief was consumed by the solar flare incinerating all in his vicinity.

Vincent's dreamline fell into the center of the dreamhub and ceased to exist. Other dreamlines joined Vincent's in their fate. Minutes later, the dream hub collapsed as well. Liberated from the hub, the hundreds of other dreamlines broke free and shot out to follow their own linear paths once again.

The six o'clock morning news started off with Manila's top story. A major fire in a thirty-story high-rise was still out of control. The reporter said the source of the fire was identified as having originated in an expensive condo owned by an up-and-coming young entrepreneur, Vincent Madarang. The cause of the fire was unknown.

CHAPTER TWELVE

The boulevard was busy at eight in the morning. Well-dressed individuals with sour faces heading toward a day of work jostled each other as they sped along the wide sidewalk. Traffic in the street crawled along at a much slower pace than the pedestrians. Construction was blocking one lane. No one noticed the extra city engineering van parked to the side. Inside, a full surveillance team was keeping tabs on their subject. The van bristled with electronic gear and a host of monitors.

Klaus was in his kitchen. One of the monitors showed him finishing his glass of orange juice, and then crossing the floor toward the living room. A second monitor picked up Klaus from the kitchen coming into the living room. He placed the glass on a table and the surveillance technician smiled as he heard the faint click of the glass making contact. The whole apartment was wired. Nothing would be missed.

"Subject leaving apartment," he said robotically into a microphone. The monitor was tagged above by a small piece of tape saying 'Body'. It showed a shaky video as Klaus walked down the hallway to the elevator. He was unaware of the ultra-miniature camera embedded in his overcoat. The slamming sound of the old fashioned elevator's outer doors made the technician wince.

Klaus walked outside his building and proceeded directly past the van and headed towards the subway. Two teams were set up, one in front and one behind him. They knew his daily routine intimately.

One thing they did not know were his thoughts. He had been planning this day over the last few nights. He had feigned sleep for hours, methodically plotting each move in his mind like a chess match. His opponents were very skilled and determined adversaries, watching every move and gesture. He could not let a suspicious glance be seen as fear or betrayal. He had decided to play it calm; business would be as usual for a few days, hopefully lulling the sentinels into a more relaxing posture.

He stopped at a mailbox and posted a letter he had written to his mother. She lived in Belgium and still never used a computer, let alone had an e-mail address. He had left instructions with her the last time that he had visited back a few weeks back. This was after he had gathered the information on Fritz. He would continue writing to her each week as he had for years and had advised that, if he stopped, she should mail the packages that he had left with her. She did not know or want to know the contents of those packages.

He continued to the stairs of the subway and as he progressed downward, an unmarked truck drove up to the mailbox. A uniformed postman opened the mailbox and the bag was emptied into the back of the truck. Two agents immediately started sorting through the mail as the truck slowly carried on. They found the envelope and skillfully opened it ensuring that no sign of damage incurred. After verifying the contents, they stopped and returned the truck to the spot where Klaus had originally dropped the letter. A couple of passers-by curiously looked on as a full mailbag was being placed back into a mailbox.

Klaus entered his office and started his day. Internal security now took over surveillance of the subject as the head agent of the CSU team contacted Ted through his SAT phone to update him.

CHAPTER THIRTEEN

Jack was seething in anger. Another e-mail from his cheating wife filled his computer screen. For˙ six years he had had to deal with her and every time the jealousy hit the pit of his stomach. Knowing that sweet piece of vindictive ass was spreading her legs for some starving artist somewhere in Brazil just kept the fire of his hatred burning.

Reading through the e-mail, he shook his head at the absurdity of her requests. The usual he thought to himself, money. Each month it was the same. All she knew was how to spend and fuck. He kept reading knowing that he didn't need to, but secretly wanting to hate her even more for leaving him.

"Bitch!" he said under his breath. He kept reading until the last paragraph, and then his eyes opened wide with shock. One word had brought the shock. Only one word that burned into his retina - divorce. It was not the thought of her finalizing the dead relationship; it was the fact that he knew she would take as much as she could from him - hundreds of millions. He was one of the most powerful and richest men in America and he was powerless to stop her. The courts would grant her what she asked for. He had expected this for six years however, he had been in complete denial, had not mentally prepared for this day.

As he looked over the vibrant city below him from his prized perched tower, his mind started to race and an idea was planted like an evil seed. Elimination was certainly in play, but the method? Should he involve Ted? Maybe only for logistics. Should he handle it personally? Jack started categorizing the details for the successful elimination.

Picking up the phone, a voice came across, "Yes sir."

"Get me a secure line to Dr. Rhinefalt in Costa Rica and have the jet ready to fly within the hour!" He hung up, not waiting for a reply, knowing his will would be done. A grin spread across his face. This was going to be a good day after all.

Nodding his head, Fritz ended the call and thought to himself; yes it is time to take it to the next stage. He thought back through his years of experimentation, through the different stages. After the war, he had escaped to South America in one of the last U-boats, carrying a fair amount of gold courtesy of the Führer, to keep him safe from prying eyes. He had kept a low profile for the first few years, writing theories and slowly acquiring equipment to start his experiments again.

The next three years involved at least one hundred subjects, mainly locals. The locals referred to him in hushed tones as Demonio, the demon. In a guarded compound, he was untouchable, never leaving its security. Local officials made sure of that. Also, having the Reich's gold behind him made things more secure for him and his work. During the war, the Führer had been very pleased with the results of Fritz's experimentation. Since Hitler was obsessed with the occult, he personally had come to witness some of Fritz's later work.

Late in the fall of 1944, the sound of motorcycles filled the quiet countryside southeast of the city of Gotha in the central Thuringen province of Germany. Four Schutzstaffel SS motorcycle riders in full uniform and regalia led the procession. Dust-covered and square-jawed, they cleared the way for the six-vehicle procession. Three were open-air staff cars, two were Tiger tanks and the last was an armored personnel carrier filled with crack Schutzstaffel SS troops, Hitler's own bodyguards. Five Luftwaffe Focke-Wulf Fw 190 fighter planes covered the skies above. The motorcade continued toward its destination deep inside Germany. The camp guards heard the engines as they echoed through the valley. The Kommandant fired orders at the honor guard in preparation for the Führer's arrival. The massive gates of the cavernous mountain research facility and factory were opened just as the motorcade arrived. Built into the mountains, such complexes served the Reich as the last hope for manufacturing and research facilities, hidden away in the heartland of Germany. They were impervious to Allied bombing, built deep into the mountain by thousands of prisoners. The conditions were inhumane and more than half the labor force would never see the light of day again.

The motorcade stopped and the Führer's personal guards jumped from their vehicles. Hitler stepped from his vehicle and was greeted by the Kommandant with a full salute. In unison, all the guards cracked their arms into a resounding "Heil Hitler!", to which he saluted back with his right hand, open-faced just up to his shoulder. After shaking the hands of the ruler of the thousand-year Reich, the Kommandant quickly led the Führer to an elevator which took them to a level five research area, far down inside the mountain.

Fritz awaited the Führer's arrival with great excitement and deep worry. The reports that he had sent to the High Command had caught the eye of the Führer himself and now was the time to validate his work. Hitler was expecting remarkable results from today's test. It had taken months of experiments and then additional weeks to perfect the techniques. Today was the day for success. The doors to the lab opened briskly, two SS guards carrying MP40 Schmeisser submachine guns leading the way. The Kommandant was explaining the details of the research facility as Hitler strode on half-listening. Seeing Fritz, he walked directly up to him, ignoring the Kommandant.

"Dr. Rhinefalt," Hitler said exuberantly and extended his hand.

Fritz excitedly gave a firm hand shake, "I'm anxious to show you my progress, Mein Führer!"

Hitler held onto the hand for longer than normal and

stared into Fritz's eyes. Fritz was far too excited to notice that Hitler was actually sizing him up. Notorious for sizing up an individual within seconds of meeting them, Hitler sensed a common kinship with this young doctor. An aura of dark evil enveloped both men. A grin came across Hitler's face and it was matched by Fritz.

The Kommandant, now off to the side, saw the grins and a chill ran down his spine. The young doctor was now protected, even before the showing of the experiment. He would have to spend more time with this doctor to garner some privileges he knew soon would be apparent.

Fritz started explaining his progress as he walked Hitler down the hall. Hitler's response, a slight nod intermittently.

"Today's experiment will validate the techniques of dream manipulation with more than one subject," Fritz mentioned as they came upon a large steel door. The two men walked into the chamber with the guards close behind, never leaving their charge. Hitler turned to the two guards and motioned with his hand for them to stay outside the chamber as the door solidly closed behind them. Fritz slipped a bolt in the door. Hitler's eyes adjusted to the dim light and he slowly took in the scene. They stopped in the center of the chamber. The air had a clean, fresh smell and the room was dead quiet. Hitler slowly turned, noticing the chambers octagonal shape with what seemed to be steel panels inset in each portion of the eight walls. Beside Fritz, a waist-high pedestal stood up from the floor with several switches and indicator lights.

"Proceed," was all Hitler said in a curious voice.

Fritz looked down to the panel and threw a switch. Immediately the eight panels slowly started receding down into the lower part of each wall. His guest's eyes widened as he looked through the eight glass panels that had been revealed. On the other side of the glass were eight small chambers each identical to the other. Each chamber, made of steel, had an access door on the far side of the room. A camera lens was situated above the glass wall pointed down toward the center of each chamber.

In the center of each chamber, a thick wire rack sat at a forty-five degree angle, sloping down toward a glass barrier. On each wire rack a man was strapped by metal restraints holding their wrists and ankles. All the men were naked and seemingly asleep.

"So far I am intrigued, Dr. Rhinefalt," Hitler quipped as he walked by each window slowly, inspecting each detail of the chambers.

"Each chamber is sound proofed from each other and equipped with both microphone and film camera to document the experiment," Fritz replied.

"How are all the subjects asleep with such bright light in the chambers?"

"I have designed a drug that relaxes the subjects and enhances the suitability to give suggestions to the subconscious mind when they are in a dream state."

"Very well, continue."

Fritz flicked a switch near a protruding microphone, "Test 168 commencing. Turning on cameras and microphones now."

Eight green lights lit up above each glass chamber.

Fritz said like a father to his son, "Mein Führer, I would be pleased if you would choose which subject I will start with."

Hitler looked back at Fritz with a smirk and said without looking away, "Lucky number seven of course."

Fritz returned the smirk and flicked the microphone switch beside the number seven on the panel. A red light came on as Fritz put his mouth to the device.

"You are part of an experiment. Do not struggle. It is early dawn, and you are situated on duty inside a concrete bunker guarding a bridge."

Fritz turned off the switch and spoke to his honored guest.

"I am only speaking to Number Seven. The other seven subjects cannot hear or see anything."

Hitler nodded again.

Fritz continued with his subject, "A battle has gone on for two hours with the enemy rapidly approaching. The temperature within the bunker starts to rise as you are now under attack by two flamethrowers."

Fritz paused to watch the reaction of Number Seven and his guest. Number Seven started to squirm in the restraints.

Fritz continued, "The flamethrowers are advancing their positions and the flame spread has almost reached the bunker. The temperature is rising to fifty degrees in your bunker."

A cry of pain emanated from the speaker of Number Seven. Hitler walked over to the window to observe more closely. Number Seven was now fighting the restraints with sweat beading throughout the subject's body.

Hitler jerked his head around at the sound of a moan coming from chamber number three. He walked over to Number Three's window and saw the subject consumed in sweat.

"Number Three can not hear Number Seven at all?" he asked.

"No, Mein Führer," Fritz answered shortly.

Fritz returned to the microphone and turned on the microphone again, "The temperature has increased another fifty degrees as the first sprays of flame touch your bunker." Fritz paused switching off the microphone again and watched as four other subjects were in the throes of pain and straining against their restraints.

Flicking the switch, Fritz continued, "One of the flamethrowers is now within range and fires a burst into the window of your bunker. Your hair starts melting and part of the flaming liquid hits your left arm."

Immediately screams of agony erupted from five rooms. Hitler turned to see the left body of Number Seven's side blistering from the imagined heat. He moved to see the other subjects and saw that nothing of this magnitude was occurring in the other chambers yet.

"The second flamethrower now fires a volley right into your bunker. The air is now molten lava and your body engulfed in an inferno."

Charred flesh was now appearing on the five subjects

and Number Three burst into flame, with the others following within seconds.

"It will soon be over," Fritz calmly announced to Hitler over the screams coming out of the chambers. All the screams slowly ceased as bodies burned in their respective chambers. Hitler turned to Fritz to make a comment when a bright flash emanated from chamber number three. Both men shielded their eyes and looked to see where it came from as an unearthly sound bellowed from the third chamber.

Fritz left the controls and stood next to the Führer to witness Number Three burning in flames. They saw something rising from the body. Something resembling a vapour trying to exit the body of the subject. The body was now charred black. The vapour being expelled resembled nothing. White bright light mixed with the flames. The unearthly sound started again and both men jumped back from the window, startled by the pitch. As they looked on, the vapour flowed to the floor and took the form of a liquid. The fluid seemed to take the shape of a hole, no - a mouth, and it was screaming out the unearthly sound. The sound continued and the form appeared to be rising as the amount of vapour increasingly flowed from the subject's body. The fluid was taking the form of the subject and a torso with arms, hands, neck and a head was becoming apparent. The subject had now become a waving, bluish white screaming entity, separate from the charred remains.

"What is that?" said Hitler in a hushed tone, his gaze mesmerized.

"This has never happened before Mein Führer," Fritz

explained.

Two arm-like forms were now reaching upward, meanwhile the sound was growing, the mouth imitating sheer agony. Suddenly the flames became more intense and the sound pitch unbearable. Both men held their heads, covering their ears and shutting their eyes tightly as they fell to their knees. The fluid form twisted around like it was trying to escape the madness.

A final scream shattered the window of the third chamber as a brilliant flash exploded also from within. Glass shards littered the floor where both Fritz and Hitler huddled. It had seemed like an eternity, but it was mere moments before the light and sound vanished. Residual smoke coming from the body entered the control chamber while the exhaust fans worked double-time to remove the stench. They both slowly rose as severe pounding on the door to the inner chamber snapped them out of their confusion.

"Leave us be!" Hitler commanded his troops through the door.

The pounding stopped and Fritz and Hitler looked at each other for a few moments in silence. A look of true admiration came across Hitler's face and then he turned to survey the room. Both men reviewed the results: five subjects charred beyond recognition, two still sleeping and Number Three in ashes. The main chamber now smelt of burnt skin and was covered in broken glass.

Hitler composed himself and walked slowly toward the controls and said, "Doctor Rhinefalt, first of all I want all your research increased and your experiments tripled. I want field experimentations to commence as soon as possible. What you have done here is one of the greatest accomplishments to the Third Reich. I will make the funds needed available for any contingency. Your work must continue!" Hitler held an outstretched hand to congratulate his newly found magician. Fritz was dumbfounded. He had thought that he would be facing a firing squad for endangering the Führer.

As Hitler held onto his grip with both hands he said, "Do you realize what we have witnessed here today? You have managed to not only control and influence dreams; you have created such a nightmare between these subjects that one of the souls was ripped from it's body. You have gone where no man has ever ventured! Doctor Rhinefalt, I commend you." Hitler's smile was immense as he continued to grip Fritz's hand and called for his guards. Fritz reached over with his left hand and unbolted the door. The Kommandant came rushing in with the troops to witness Hitler's embrace with Fritz.

"Doctor Rhinefalt," said the Kommandant still watching the shaking of hands, "we had three prisoners combust into flames inside the prisoner's sleeping area two levels up."

Hitler released Fritz and headed towards the door. As the guards followed, Hitler stopped and looked back at Fritz, "Next, the world!"

CHAPTER FOURTEEN

Jack circled the Zicon compound in Costa Rica. As the helicopter started its descent, Jack spied a newly built small building on the far end of the compound, away from the main buildings. Ted had not reported this and he was slightly put off when he exited the landed helicopter.

Ted stood by the tarmac and saw the scowl on Jack's face. Wonderful, he thought, knowing there was a blast coming.

"What the hell is that new building, Ted? I explicitly asked to be notified on all activities taking place here," Jack yelled trying to be heard over the winding down helicopter.

Ted internally felt like rolling his eyes. "Jack, Fritz had that building erected in the last two days. It was slated to be put on your daily report today."

"All right, all right," Jack waved his hands as if to get on with it.

"It is part of Fritz's latest test that he is ready to show you," Ted spoke while leading Jack to a small golf cart. They climbed in and Ted drove toward the small building.

They drove in silence and Jack looked beyond the fence to the hundreds of teak trees surrounding the compound.

Might be a good locale to set up more operations. Very secluded, he concluded.

A warm breeze with the salty scent from the ocean passed through them. Ted stopped in front of the unimpressive building. It was a small thirty-by-thirty stucco single-story hut. Another golf cart was off to the side. As they walked in, Jack's eyes momentarily went blank from the bright glare to the almost pitch black interior. An inside door with a green light above opened and Fritz came out.

It was Jack's first meeting with Fritz. He sized up the man quickly. Ted made the introductions and Jack was surprised by the strength of the firm handshake from such an elderly man.

Fritz started right in, "First of all, I have replicated all my earlier experiments using drugs to induce suggestions into the subjects who are in dream states. This again has proved effective on influencing the dreams of the subjects and, in later experiments, groups of other subjects in close proximity to the affected subjects."

Jack still dumbfounded that this was actually happening asked, "So Dr. Rhinefalt, how is it possible that others are affected as well?" Ted stood to the side and was shocked that Jack had used Fritz's last name. Knowing Jack for so many years, he knew that few men warranted this kind of respect from Jack.

Fritz's face took on a glow from being asked about his work, "Well, I can only postulate at this point, but from my hundreds of tests, I had one subject that was affected from being in close proximity and still lived for a half hour after the rest of them had died. I questioned him and it seemed that he had been dreaming normally and then, as if being struck, his dream jumped into a nightmarish scenario. The very same scenario that I had induced in the main subjects. He described a sense being caught in a spiral that prevented him from escaping this nightmare. He was a very strong-willed subject I must add. He told me that he fought the dream, trying to get a foothold on reality, almost clawing his way back up a descending evil spiral. Somehow he successfully fought the nightmare and broke free from the scenario. He awoke but was so badly burnt from the effects of the original nightmare that he soon passed on after we spoke."

"Absolutely incredible," Jack said staring at Fritz.

Fritz continued, "So from this, an enlightened theory has been forming in my mind. The nightmare spiral was sort of a dreamhub. Then with its negative energy, it grew and became a faster spiral. Any dreamers near this hub would be pulled toward the hub, thus feeding the negative energy. The spiral would continue feeding until all were consumed and then physically dead. I also suspect that since the dreams are artificially started, this accelerates the spiral and that is what causes the physical transformation. The subjects have no chance to disbelieve that this is actually happening to them."

Jack jumped in excitedly, "Tapping right into their subconscious then."

"Exactly, Mr. Montgomery. Right into their psyche

and, as I observed back in 1944, their soul," Fritz turned and headed back inside the interior door. Jack and Ted simply followed, Jack almost beside himself to see what was inside.

"This last month," Fritz continued, "I have been trying to recreate the experiments that I did in the 60s and 70s involving different delivery methods to induce the subjects. Mr. Montgomery, drugs worked extremely well, but this limits the use of this method to really just capturing and injecting a subject. I could not remotely induce a subject from a distance. Even if we did somehow inject the drug into a subject without their knowing, how would we give them the proper suggestion and imagery for the subject to start its own negative dreamhub?"

"So Doctor, I presume that since you had this building erected far from the others, you have perfected this different delivery method?" Jack smiled with a sinister turn of the lip.

Fritz nodded, "I have done one initial test. I have made some modifications. The equipments these days are much more powerful and accurate."

Jack had not even noticed that they had been speaking in complete darkness since entering the room. Jack jumped when Fritz flipped on the interior light. A local Costa Rican female was strapped to a metal chair with straps on her forehead, wrists and ankles. Jack followed the slim ankles upward and stopped for quick glance at the patch between her legs and his gaze fell on her ample breasts. Her mouth was open, drool coming out of the left side.

"A local prostitute," Fritz pointed out. "We have sound,

camera and electrodes hooked up to monitor her vital signs and brain activity."

"Has she been drugged?" Jack asked, looking again at her mound.

"No, she has been kept awake for seventy-two hours and she has then been allowed to fall into a deep sleep."

Fritz started walking out the door. Again, Jack and Ted simply followed, mesmerized by Fritz's presence. Fritz closed up the exterior door and then climbed into one of the golf carts and started away toward the other buildings.

Jack looked at Ted and said, "That man has no conscience. It is all one experiment to him."

Ted nodded as they watched the demon rapidly gain distance from them.

Inside the air-conditioned research building, a chill ran down Jack's spine. Was it the air conditioning or was it what he was to witness? Ted had left a few minutes earlier stating that he had security arrangements to oversee. In fact, Ted did not want to witness another of Fritz's experiments. The last had been horrific enough, with the subject named Manuel trying to speak of his experiences in his dying breaths. How Manuel had survived that last half an hour would burn into Ted's mind forever. Burnt to a crisp, the poor man was somehow still capable of a raspy disjointed reflection to his torturer.

Jack could sense that Ted was not up to his usual effectiveness. He mentally made a note to contact his special operative William Su, his spy of spies, to get the inside scoop on what might be affecting him.

Fritz snapped Jack back to the present, "This is where we'll monitor the progress." Fritz pointed to a bank of monitors. All five cameras had been placed at different angles to capture all movements of the subjects.

Fritz continued on, "In the 60's and 70's I experimented with radio waves. Bombarding a subject with specific images and sounds."

"Hang on!" Jack jumped in, "They are asleep. What good would images be?"

Fritz took his question in stride. "The waves act more like broadcast television. The subjects do not actually see the images, but since the waves are directly pointed toward them, they are engulfed in the energy of the wave. The waves are composed of negative still images and clips of movies and, as the wave continues, our subjects are deeply affected by their negative energy."

As Fritz paused, Jack knew that the cold he was feeling was not from the air conditioning in the room.

"And now," he continued, "with the generous funding of your company," and Fritz graciously nodded his head towards Jack who reciprocated with a nod, "I have been able to take this to a new level. With a few adjustments, I have successfully been able to bombard a subject with a stream of images and sounds a hundred more times more powerful than with the radio waves." Fritz stopped to sip a fresh cup of coffee

"Well please don't stop now, Dr. Rhinefalt," Jack said eagerly.

"I have done this now with microwaves. An intense beam of digital images and sounds is directed right at the subject. The last experiment was done in this building from one room to another. It worked very well. Now I wish to test a true long-distance experiment over the compound. If this is successful, barring technical issues of directional focus and the strength of the beam, I should be able to induce subjects over long distances."

"How long of a distance?" Jack asked quietly.

"As long as we have the line of sight, I could see us using this as far away as the horizon is from us," Fritz said proudly.

Jack took a seat at the monitors and only said two words, "Go ahead."

Fritz nodded and started working a control panel. He worked in silence for two minutes and then pointed at a monitor placed beside the one giving a close-up frontal view of the woman.

"This monitor will show you the images that are being beamed to her. The stream is looped so that all the images will repeat once per minute at the start, making it easier for us to construct the scenario. The image stream starts slow and then speeds up, which will intensify the nightmare spiral. I would strongly suggest that you stop looking at the monitor after a couple of minutes."

Jack looked up from the monitor and switched his gaze to Fritz. He watched Fritz's facial expressions as he completed the preparations. Jack was amazed that Fritz could remain so expressionless. A true killing machine, he thought. The image monitor came alive. Jack stared as it flickered a couple of times. The sound of a steadily increasing whine started. He looked back to see a small disk pointed outside the now open window.

"The microwave dish, I presume?" he asked.

"Yes, and it is warming up. We shall begin the stream in thirty seconds."

Jack returned his gaze to the monitors only to start squirming in his chair. The image monitor was now playing. Jack had read in his reports about the subjects having spontaneously combusted, but he was not prepared for these images.

The one-minute movie started its loop again. A movie showing millions of ants filled the screen, ants as far as the eye could see. A man was stumbling through the sea of ants. As he stumbled along, the ants attacked him. He fought them off in vain. A close up of his face showed his eyes being eaten and the rest of his face quickly covered. His legs were now in the picture, the ants biting his exposed flesh. The man fell into the swarm and was engulfed, dying a horrendous death. The one-minute movie started once again. A scream from the speaker switched Jack's focus to the next monitor. The girl strained against her restraints. Her mouth tightly closed as though trying to stop the ants from entering her mouth. Jack switched to another monitor that showed a close up of her legs and that perfect mound.

"Stream now at fifty percent," Fritz stated flatly.

Jack's eyes widened as he started to see the flesh of the girl starting to change. Blood started seeping from dozens of new openings. Her skin rippled in different directions as if she were being ravaged by real ants.

The screaming started again, this time with no conscious effort to keep her mouth closed. She had an uninhibited expression of anguish. Jack was spellbound. He sat back to watch all the monitors at once.

"Seventy-five percent," Fritz stated flatly. The images were now almost a blur. The minute video was now a fifteen-second show.

The girl was a mess of flesh and blood. Her body was trying to sway back and forth when Jack spied a glowing form lingering each time the girl swayed in the other direction.

"What the hell is that?" Jack pointed to the monitor showing the frontal view.

Fritz looked at the same monitor and said slowly, "It is her soul trying to escape the madness."

Jack, with his mouth agape, watched as the form grew, now overtaking the lifeless, silent body. An unholy sound started to rise from the still swaying body, and, in a brilliant flash, the room turned into a supernova-like explosion. Jack fell backward in his chair and stared at Fritz. He said nothing for a full thirty seconds.

"All we need is a line of sight?" he said now kneeling beside the chair.

"Yes," was Fritz's reply, still looking at the monitors.

"Would a line of site from a satellite work?" Jack asked with huge eyes.

Fritz, for the first time in years, started grinning.

CHAPTER FIFTEEN

The table in front of them was set for two. The main dishes had been cleared and dark Costa Rican coffee steamed from large mugs. Jack dipped his spoon into his dessert of fried bananas smothered in a sweet sour cream. He made a wish to himself to have this incredible taste imported back home. Jack also thought how challenging it was to draw Fritz into a conversation.

He had met many private and closed individuals, but Fritz was really one of a kind. If not prompted, he would not have said one word over dinner. Time to get back to business, he thought.

"As I stated before, I can provide satellite coverage pretty much anywhere. What I need to know from you is if you can you achieve the same effect from a satellite." Jack finished by taking a sip from his mug.

"A satellite will have more than enough power to deliver the microwave signal to the surface. The challenge will be in concentrating the beam into a narrow band that can be focused on a single individual," Fritz answered as if he had been speaking about it for an hour.

Jack pondered the point for a minute, and sipped his

coffee again. He raised his eyes to reply to Fritz and was met by a steady stare.

A chill ran down Jack's spine again. This guy is downright dangerous, he thought.

Jack continued, "We need to do a test. From there we can have a point of reference to fine-tune the beam. I have a target in mind within a nearby satellite range."

Fritz raised an eyebrow at that comment. He had been trying to judge Jack's level of commitment to the project. Would he be able to stomach the next phase? The answer was yes. He had just heard the affirmative. Fritz nodded at Jack to continue.

Jack swallowed hard and said, "The target is a woman in a small town in Brazil. There will probably be a male with her. I wish to have both targeted." He stopped, setting in motion his wife's demise.

"From your expression, this woman was once close to you," Fritz replied in his usual cold manner.

"The identity does not concern you," Jack spat back. "I want anyone in that dwelling taken care of. I will place units of surveillance at the location prior to the event to record and measure the effectiveness."

The lighting in the room changed as the sun set, sending strange shadows across Fritz's face. Fritz was not about to let go of the small irritant that he had started.

"Would it not be wise to pick another target to practice on rather than start with a target so sensitive?" Fritz smiled inwardly, "It is certainly possible that things may go awry in the first satellite beaming."

Jack, now irritated, fumbled at cutting a cigar and

took a deep breath. He re-sliced the cigar and slowly lit it while calming his nerves. He knew that Fritz had found a vulnerable spot and he had to take back control of the conversation. Taking a long drag and exhaling, he started again with renewed strength.

"Herr Rhinefalt, from what I saw today, I am certain that it will work. You will not let it fail. It was your crowning moment in over fifty years of work. That is not the issue."

Jack tapped the cigar and held it in his left hand, looking directly into Fritz's eyes. The smoke slowly built a thin barrier between them.

"It will work and I will protect what time you have left on this planet to live in quiet luxury. You can guess the other side of the equation," Jack continued to stare at Fritz for ten seconds before leaning back and looking out the window while enjoying another delicious drag of his cigar.

Fritz continued to stare at Jack's turned head. Fear was not the emotion flowing through him, but amusement. For Fritz, being on this planet mattered not. He would have left a long time ago, but he could not willfully take his own life. Oh yes, he would conduct Jack's bidding and take his trinkets of luxury if only to prolong his growing contempt for the man. This technology could be better utilized to change the hierarchy of the world, not for one man's personal vengeance. However, a vengeance seed had already started to sprout in Fritz's mind. Fritz picked up his napkin and while wiping his mouth hid for the second time that day a small grin.

CHAPTER SIXTEEN

A few days later the CSU team of three slipped through the back alley of a row of hastily built houses and came up to a clearing. They were within sight of their objective. Near the edge of the town a small but expensive villa rested on a hill, secluded from the rest by over a half acre of immaculate rock gardens and small trees. It truly was a place of wealth, overlooking the rest of the town of Cabo Frio on the Brazilian coast. The three came up to a row of small trees and stopped to check out their surroundings. The sound of water filled the silence as an artificial waterfall in front of the villa gurgled, making the team leader smile. More than he could ask for, lots of cover and ambient noise to camouflage their movements. They approached the villa cautiously. Closer to the villa, at about one hundred feet, they came across a rock formation that would shield them from view. The team leader looked at his watch. One twenty in the morning. He caught the eyes of one of his teammates and nodded. His teammate nodded back and proceeded toward the villa.

Moving stealthily like a cat, he reached the outside

wall and pulled out a small PDA and accessed the villa's schematics. Ivan had been up to his old tricks again for Ted and had found the villas blueprints stored in an architect's computer in Rio de Janeiro. Finding the main bedroom on the drawing, he closed the program and crawled around the corner and stopped. Luck was with him tonight. There was an open window to the main bedroom. He would not have to drill tonight.

Opening his equipment satchel, he took out a micro camera and microphone. Anyone seeing it would have thought it was a very thin snake. The other end was comprised of a transmitter device that transmitted to the team leader one hundred feet away. He slowly placed the camera over the windowsill and turned it on.

The team leader already had the receiver unit on when the picture appeared. The picture was of a dresser against a wall. The audio was another matter. The sounds of moaning filled the ear cups of his headset. The targets were definitely in the house. He quietly instructed the camera operator to adjust the angle. The picture panned to the left to reveal two naked bodies on a bed. No sheets. They were on the floor. The targets were in the midst of a full on love session, with the male thrusting into the female from behind. The team leader instructed the camera operator to stay at his post and to adjust if the subjects moved. The third operative was busy connecting the satellite feed to the video receiver. Once the satellite feed was ready, he started transmitting.

Back in Costa Rica, Jack and Fritz sat in front of the monitors waiting for the satellite video connection. Abruptly it came on with the room exploding in sound that had not been adjusted since the last experiment. Jack sat with an expression of shock as he watched his wife getting the fuck of her life. Fritz was also surprised, but was enjoying Jack's reaction. He did not even attempt to turn down the volume, turning back to the video screen. The couple was now switching positions as the male lay on the bed and the woman was bouncing up and down on top of him. The male had sat up and engulfed a nipple with his mouth. His hands were now on her wriggling ass shoving her down even harder on his cock with each stroke. She arched her back and let out a primal scream. Jack was beside himself. He had not planned on this. The plan was to execute the beam at two in the morning. Looking at his watch, it was one forty-five. They both needed to be asleep for the beam to take effect.

Jealousy engulfed him as he continued to watch his wife ride her Latin lover. He could tell from her moves that she was riding a much larger cock than his. She had never screamed like that with him. He just sat there with a black cloud over him. Fritz said nothing, enjoying the show. She was a very beautiful woman and very agile. The minutes passed, as did the positions.

The team leader looked at his watch again and began to worry. It was two thirty now and the targets were not looking like they were going to stop anytime soon. He should be gathering the camera back and heading to the extraction point now. He had turned down the sound. The screams and moans from the woman were distracting his work. He laughed to himself. He knew their fate once they fell asleep and was glad they were enjoying their last session.

At three thirty, Jack could almost take no more. He looked up briefly to watch the spectacle of his ex-wife on her hands and knees, her perfectly shaped ass high in the air being rammed non stop by her stud with the sound of body parts quickly slapping together. Both were silent for once, the stud with a determined expression to fuck the hell out of her and she had her mouth open in a silent scream, her eyes ready to pop. Jack gazed back down just as a primal earthy long moan finally escaped her. He remembered that their love sessions had lasted half an hour max. He closed his eyes, shook his head and raised his hand to his forehead. This is the worst night of my life, he thought.

At four o'clock the couple lay spooning together, the male still inside the female. A look of pure bliss was on her face. By four fifteen the targets were finally quiet.

Fritz leaned over and flicked a switch. A time window popped up on the team leaders view screen, showing a fifteen-minute countdown.

Jack had not even spoken through the whole sordid episode. For the next few minutes he thought back to the few good moments with his wife, which then turned to hateful moments. Years of hate and abandonment. He watched the countdown silently with Fritz. When it reached zero, he looked over to Fritz and nodded.

Fritz looked back to the control panel and pressed a bright yellow button. A second monitor turned on above the video monitor from Brazil. The images started their slow rotation: pictures of fire, heat and death in the consuming flames. These images were up-linked to a waiting Zicon satellite over the equator. The satellite, acting like a relay, did not care about the content of the images, its sole purpose to do the bidding of its controllers. There had been a small calculation error when uploading the destination parameters of the downlink beam to the villa. The beam shot out of the satellite and down to the planet. The parameter for this first beam was an area of one hundred square feet centered on the villa and the surrounding land on the hilltop. This would take care of the guesthouse as well, if the targets had been in there.

When the beam hit, the team leader shuddered as the energy was hitting his body also. Within three minutes, sounds came through his headset. Looking at his view screen, he saw that the two targets were still locked in a spoon, his cock still inside her, but they were now both moaning from the effects of the beam. The moans became more intense and the team leader watched emotionless as he saw the two start turning red and blistering. You would think that the two people in agony would have fought to separate themselves, to get away from any physical touch that would intensify their torment. Unbeknownst to Jack or Fritz, the two were in the most intense dreaming experience of their lives, actually the most intense wet dream. So strong was their love for each other that as the negative dreamhub pulled them in closer and the heat increased, their bodies burned like a new log being thrown on a raging bonfire. Mentally they felt no pain, just pure love. They were glued to each other now face to face, his cock deep inside her thrusting like a piston while her legs were wrapped around his waist, her feet resting on his buttocks. The ultimate lingering kiss muffled their moans. They started clawing each other as even the feelings became too intense.

Jack leaned forward on the edge of his chair, his chin resting on his arms and watched his beautiful wife start to melt, the two lovers now joined by flesh as each grabbed each other as if they were one. Seeing his ex die horribly should have brought him delight, yet he still felt jealousy run through him as he saw their bodies move to a sexual crescendo while dying. After ten minutes they stopped moving, definitely dead. Two ethereal forms rose over the charred bodies and the unearthly moaning started. This time the two forms melded into one, the face changing from his wife's to the Latin lover's. The tempo and sound became intense. The team outside the villa winced as the sound reached their ears, resonating all around them.

Fritz shut off the beam at this point, his mission completed. Back at the villa, windows began to shatter in the night as the sound became almost unbearable. The team leader looked at the villa and saw shattered glass everywhere. His team member at the villa was running back toward the control point holding a bloodied arm from a shard of glass. He looked back at the video screen only to be momentarily blinded as a brilliant flash erupted from the screen. The villa blew outward as if it had been rigged with explosives. The team was protected by the large rocks surrounding them as pieces of the villa fell from the sky. Flames now licked out from the villa's foundation. All stealthiness had evaporated as the team was already heading out back through the property's tree line when they stopped in astonishment. There were dozens of homes in flames, the streets were in chaos. Homes outside the range of the beam were also aflame. The sound of emergency vehicles saturated the air.

The team leader quickly assessed the situation and decided to head back through the villa property, to the other side of the hill. As they circled around the still burning villa, the sky was red with the glow of the fires. Coming over the crest of the hill and looking down, they saw that sheer pandemonium now ruled as rows and rows of apartment blocks were alight. The scene was unimaginable, a firestorm raged in the valley encompassing six square blocks of low-end ten-story housing units. Dozens of buildings looked as though they were roman candles completely engulfed in flames. Residents were now jumping out of windows only to be consumed in the firestorm that ran its course throughout the neighborhood.

One of the team members began to vomit from the sheer shock of what they had unleashed. The heat was becoming unbearable as the firestorm grew, while in the background noise of the fire the screams of people dying was unmistakable. The team leader looked to see if there was an escape route on the side of the high hill. The firestorm was coming up the hill fed by the winds and dense undergrowth. The team moved to the left side of the hill only to find a similar scene, the air growing hotter. The team leader sent his two-team members to the other sides of the hill to check out their predicament. Each reported a similar scene, the firestorm now surrounding their hill and climbing. The leader ordered them back to the position facing the apartments. Knowing his fate, the team leader pulled out his view screen computer and typed a quick final report.

'Targets neutralized. Beam area seems to be ten times to parameter setting. Hundreds of homes effected.... Firestorm now ensuing. Team trapped on hilltop...No chance of escape....'

The firestorm continued to grow and reach up the hill. The two-team members came running back with sweat pouring off their faces and stood looking at the leader who had an expression that both members understood. They looked at each other once and nodded. The team leader looked at each man as he pulled the trigger of his silenced pistol. He took one last look around, placed the barrel to his head and yelled, "Next!" as he pulled the trigger once more.

CHAPTER SEVENTEEN

Tony Blake accessed his personal e-mail on one of Peter's desk stations at the lab. After typing in his user name and password, the e-mails that he normally accessed in Tokyo started to appear on the web browser.

Amazing, he thought, how far the world has come in the last few years. Among all the spam, an e-mail caught his eye from Encryptnow, an encrypted e-mail provider. Clicking on the e-mail, it stated that it needed a key to further open the e-mail. A hint word was attached: CONFERENCE. Tony stared at the monitor for a few seconds and then slightly chuckled to himself. Klaus!

Tony typed in 'KLAUS'; 'That is not the correct password' was the reply.

"Was this Klaus?" he thought.

Nancy walked behind him with some coffee and offered, "Any coffee there, Tex?"

Tony whipped his head around and exclaimed, "Brilliant!" with a huge smile. He immediately went back to the keyboard and typed 'Texas' remembering that Klaus had remarked on his being from the big state.

Nancy, oblivious to this, kind of smirked and shrugged her shoulders and started pouring a cup for Tony. Leaning over and placing the cup at his side, she looked over his shoulder at the screen. It was half filled with text and the bottom part of the page filled with the top of an old photo.

"My god," she gasped, "what is that?"

Tony slowly turned his head towards her, their noses almost touching as the rest of the report came on the screen with the digital photos. Nancy did not move back. She stared into Tony's eyes, not with any desire, but with remorse at what she had just seen.

"Please tell me that this has stopped," she said quietly.

Tony's lips pressed together and he slowly shook his head.

The three of them sat behind a small conference table sorting through the text pages and photos that Tony had printed out.

"These have to be the most sadistic war crimes yet," Peter exclaimed, pulling some photos from a pile.

"I don't know if I want to dream again," Nancy quipped.

They had read through the meticulous reports of Fritz's experiments that, with Nazi efficiency, reported all the details, times, reactions, methods used and documented.

Tony broke in, "Well over a hundred tests and then the project vanished. Somehow the reports were not given the same fate."

"Yes, but Klaus eluded that they, what was that name again?" he shuffled through some papers and found the proper one. "Zicon," he continued, "they found this doctor alive and well, and he has started this madness again."

"To what end?" Nancy asked. "I mean why would anyone or a corporation want to be associated with this, this...," pointing at the screen, shaking her head

"Christ, who knows these days," Peter said with distress. "This world is out of control. A rogue country or dictator, a dishonest or environmentally destructive corporation, they are all the same. Power," he paused, "power and the bottom line is what they want. Most are above the law anyway."

Tony nodded, "Very sad but true. So the question remains on the table," he paused, "Klaus has taken a huge risk sending this to us. Actually to me. We now know that Zicon knows about your research. Kind of surreal actually that it came through me. Anyway, we know that Fritz's experiments are also back online."

"Also," Nancy jumped in, "that Klaus knows that he is being watched."

"Yes," Tony nodded, "our only contact has to be very careful. We may never receive more info."

Peter sat back and crossed his arms and slowly nodded his head, "Well then, I guess we better set up a test and see if we can find or make one of these dreamhubs that Fritz is talking about."

"We can't subject anyone to these types of tests!" Nancy said with her mouth agape, sliding her hand over the photos.

"Who said anything about nightmares?" Peter winked at her.

Jason and his crew had been on a long voyage coming around Cape Horn across the South Atlantic and were a hundred nautical miles south of Rio de Janeiro. The journey had been a difficult one because of the rough seas and the crew was looking forward to some well-deserved shore leave. Not a large vessel, the hundred and fifty foot motor yacht held a crew of eight relatively young seamen learning the ropes on this cruise.

"Captain, we have a distress call on the radio," the radioman announced. "They state that they are taking on water and need assistance."

"Very well, how far out are they?" was the reply.

"I have them on radar bearing 0280 degrees, twenty nautical miles away."

"Ok, make for the ship, best speed, and hail them that we are responding." Just lovely he thought, shaking his head. Land will have to wait a little longer.

Sixty minutes later, Jason's vessel came along side a fifty-foot older wooden motor yacht. Jason's eyes opened wide when he saw the passengers on the rail of the listing ship. Eight drop dead gorgeous women.

"Holy shit!" was all the second in command said. Luckily the ocean was calmer that evening so the crew made short of tying the boats together and getting the women and their belongings into their vessel. Jason had never seen his crew all smiles while working before. He too started smiling as a beautiful, tall brunette walked over and introduced herself as the skipper of the ailing boat, which was taking on water through a rotting keel. It would have never made it back to shore.

After finding out they were professional models on a trip back from one of the nearby beaches for a photo shoot, Jason invited all to the galley below as nightfall was approaching. Since the ship was mostly run by computers, the crew was not taking no for an answer to join the women below. Sixteen bodies in the lower mess cabin and kitchen made it snug, just the way Jason wanted it to be. The room was about two hundred square feet in size, a large and sturdy ten-person table centered the room, with short backed chairs circled around. This made the room even smaller and Jason smiled as he looked around the room at his crew. Bottles of wine and rum came out of nowhere as the crew broke out the precious supplies they had been holding for some special celebration. The women were not alarmed or concerned, quite the opposite. The young crew was around their own age, very rugged and willing to please. As the night progressed, electronic trance music pumped through the sound system and sixteen capsules of ecstasy, courtesy of one of the girls, now lay on the table surrounded by the group. Each one took one of the capsules and held them to their mouths. They gave each other a knowing look as one yelled, "Down the hatch!" and they all swallowed the pleasure pills.

The group started mingling and flirting, all of them knowing where this was heading. Within half an hour, the pills had kicked in and things started heating up. The crew tried to move the table for more room, but it had been securely anchored to the floor in case of ship sway. The energy and atmosphere of the room built up from the usual getting to know someone to intimate details of past experiences. One of the crew walked over to the ship's music system and chose some seductive house music with a beat that grew and grew. The girls started dancing with each other and the crew readily joined in. Two of the girls, a hot little Latin number and a fiery red head climbed on top of the table and began to start a slow and tantalizing dance nose to nose. The two males left alone, leaned against one of the walls, cold beers in their hands and lust in their eyes. They watched the two girls start to caress each other intimately through the sheer clothing, as it was such a hot night out. A moan escaped the redhead as the other's hand stroked the now wet spot between her tanned legs. The redhead grabbed the back of the Latin girl's head and proceeded to give her a deep long kiss. The music now had a rhythmic beat that went deep into the sub-conscious, the music of passion. You could smell the pheromones flying through the room, Jason thought as the tall brunette started stroking the bulging package in his pants.

Within minutes clothing was coming off both sexes. The two girls were now prone in a 69 position on the table in a full out oral exploration of each other. The two guys on the sidelines had had enough and joined the girls on the table. Other couples formed, fondling each other only to be touched by others right beside them. The group moved as one, each in its own ecstasy of the moment only to be heightened by a new partner or partners switching back and forth, side to side. The soft moaning of the crew and girls became louder as the tempo of the music, passion and lust grew.

Nancy and Tony watched as Peter was smiling ear-to-ear sitting in his chair. Tony looked over at Nancy and noticed her intense gaze toward Peter. He followed her gaze to Peter's crotch eyeing the tent in his pants. Tony shook his head, smiled and turned around to face the sixteen college students lying in their cots all squirming around.

"Can you feel that?" Nancy asked, also grinning ear-to-ear.

"Oh ya," Tony replied, trying not to get a tent of his own in his shorts.

"It worked. It really worked," she said.

"We should look at the computer model being created," Tony said as he walked around the table to look at a monitor. Nancy was still looking at Peter with a smile on his face. Only in your dreams, she thought when she heard Tony do a low whistle.

She walked over and faced the monitor. It was now displaying several white lines which were spiraling in a clockwise motion toward a small center. The lines were increasing in speed just as moans of pleasure started erupting from the students on the cots. The energy in the room was almost supercharged. Nancy unknowingly linked her fingers with Tony's. Tony, somewhat oblivious to this, was mesmerized by the screen and the results of the new software he had just programmed. They were witnessing true interaction of dreams.

Two of the students who were now having the time of their lives were brilliant software programmers. They were in their final year at MIT. Within three days of a development meeting with Peter, Nancy and Tony, they utilized Tony's knowledge of brain response. Using an outline of the dreamweave process, they created a software program that was light-years ahead of anything else out there: being able to link images from the subconscious of one to another only while the test subject was unaware, ensuring true inhibitions.

The hair on the back of Nancy's neck bristled because of the screams of ecstasy and orgasms now erupting from the group. She felt Tony's fingers tighten. Suddenly, all that was heard was soft moaning from the group. Their fingers released from each other as their composure returned. Tony gazed into the monitor as the spiral slowed and one by one the lines started off onto their own direction away from the hub.

Peter walked up beside them, a satisfied look on his face. Nancy noticed that he was holding his lab coat closed, covering the front and hiding a wet stain on his khakis.

"Well, that was most interesting," Peter said smugly.

"Ah huh," Nancy smiled. "Probably won't have any problems getting volunteers for this again."

"What did you see?" Tony asked punching keys on the keyboard.

Peter explained that it was like watching a movie as he had been connected to the initial subject Jason, who had been isolated by glass from the others. Peter was a spectator in Jason's dream, going along but not able to participate. They had also utilized newly engineered software from Tony's theoretical work and experimentation attempts on the neutral network mapping. Basically, the ability for one individual to be able to tap into and view images of another. Tony had kept his work very secret over the last few years for fears of it getting into the wrong hands. Peter's experiment was the first live test out of Tony's lab in Japan and he was smiling inside at its success. Nancy tried to hide her sexual energy quickening again as Peter finished describing the last moments of the ship's tale.

"Oh, you have to see this," Tony spoke up, not taking his eyes off the monitor. Peter and Nancy looked down and watched.

"Ok, this is the start and I have sped up the display by four times. This is Jason's dreamline." Tony pointed to a white line extending from the bottom of the large 21-inch monitor as the visual playback of the dreamweave software started again.

"See how it is a linear line. Now this is when we introduced the scenario to Jason." Tony added as he looked at the time counter in the bottom right hand of the screen. They had simply played an audio clip to Jason when he had hit REM giving him a nudge in the direction of the dream they wanted him to have. Further along, more audio was introduced adding, to the emotion of the situation. Nancy chuckled at the memory of the suggestion she had made of using a simple method of playing a steamy section of a Harlequin Romance audio book. What was even funnier was when Nancy showed up the next day with not one but four audio books from her own collection. She had shrugged at the sarcastic comments from both men, shook her head and said, "Men."

"Now watch from the left as another dreamline appears. Again, here is a linear line slightly parallel to Jason's. Do you see that?" Tony said expectantly. "It is starting to curve towards Jason's line."

For the next few minutes they watched as Jason's line stopped moving forward and started spinning clockwise. The second dreamline started joining Jason's in the same spiral but not touching. After ten minutes fourteen other lines were spinning around each other, starting to concentrate toward the center. The lines were now a blur, each line melding into one, the spiral closing in on itself. Finally, a white flash appeared in the center forcing all the lines to break free and head off into new directions again in a linear fashion. The orgasmic dream finished and the dreamhub energy dissipated.

Peter looked up to see Nancy helping the subjects unhook from the wires and was amused at the embarrassed faces of the young students, especially the males all with stains on their pants. The group slowly exited all aglow and shaking their heads, thanking Nancy for the twenty-dollar fee they had just earned. They were ecstatic to come back, needed or not.

Nancy locked the door and came back to the two still analyzing the data.

"Well," she said with her arms crossed and a mischievous look on her face, "I was offered $100 to do this again. Want to start a new venture or have a fundraiser?"

Tony and Peter both erupted into laughter.

CHAPTER EIGHTEEN

Klaus waited a week, going through the motions but cautiously inventorying his own company's surveillance on himself. He had waited for the hammer to fall earlier in the week when he had slipped into an Internet café after losing his tail for a few minutes. He had opened his Encryptnow account and uploaded the files and images from his portable flash drive, the new millennium's floppy disk, and attached them to his e-mail to Tony. He had not had the chance to see if Tony had received the e-mail, but no CSU agents had knocked down his door, yet. This did not mean that Klaus was free and clear, far from it.

He was being watched 24/7 except for the ten minutes in the café that he had given himself. He had walked out of the café with a cappuccino in hand ready to return to his apartment, knowing full well that it was blanketed in audio and video devices belonging to the team that followed him to work each and every day. So he decided to have some fun with them when he could.

One night Klaus spotted a man and woman surveillance team. He decided out of the blue to walk into a XXX movie house and watch a full movie. He purposely sat near the front, so that the agents would have to be near him to keep close. Klaus had not looked at the movie bill announcing what was playing and was laughing to himself for the next two hours as it proved to be a series of short clips of absolute perverse sexual footage on just about anything you could think of. As he left he saw the disgusted look on the female agent's face.

His only free time to himself was at the office. Since Zicon was a well-secured building, surveillance was very light, but when he left the building, the company resumed its job. Being in charge of Zicon's research and development in Germany, Klaus was privy to many secrets. Dark secrets that he knew he could vanish for, but he did not intend to vanish by the hands of Zicon. He had, over the years, compiled dozens of top-secret information packages that would put Zicon and its executives at the top of any hit list for Interpol and American military authorities. Zicon had, through Jack's direction, branched into many grey areas of the world. Through a myriad of holding companies and numbered accounts in private banks, Jack had control of assets of over a hundred billion dollars. Weapon systems, biochemistry, satellite development, surveillance and legitimate enterprises such as shipping in the Indian Ocean, to theatre companies in South America. The packages outlined that Zicon and the holding companies did not care whom they sold information to. Someone was always willing to pay the price for a satellite shot of their neighboring country's various military assets. Many of the so-called free world leaders would not be too pleased if they had such dossiers.

Klaus had over the years copied and hidden multiple copies in bank safe deposits in Hamburg and Zurich. A couple of close friends had envelopes to open upon his death or mysterious disappearance. The executive at Zicon suspected it, so Klaus was safe from a quick demise, at least temporarily.

He left his office at the end of the day and a new team started their daily routine of 'seek and hide'. He followed the same trek back towards his apartment but, unknown to them, the information he carried in his briefcase guaranteed that he would never step back into his apartment again. If they found out what was inside the case he would be running for the rest of his days. He had feared that he would not get out of the office before being found out.

Klaus had planned his escape now for a few weeks, working out all the fine points to vanish in broad daylight. He walked along the street to his usual subway entrance, taking his time to keep his 'friends' behind him. Waiting on the platform for the subway train, he turned and walked purposefully directly towards them. The female agent was flustered and gave a quick glance to her tall male counterpart. The male agent slipped his right hand in his overcoat, gripping the handle of his pistol, preparing himself for his subject's next move. Klaus walked straight at them, avoiding eye contact. Within two meters, the female agent also went for her gun. Both showed their lack of experience in the field, as this was one of their first assignments. Klaus changed direction slightly and started to go between the two agents. The roar of the subway train started to fill the emptiness of the station. Both agents started to pull their pistols as Klaus excused himself and reached for a discarded newspaper on the seat behind them. Klaus quickly turned around and headed back toward the edge of the platform as the cars swiftly went by. A slight smirk appeared on his lips at the rattling of his foe.

Getting off at his usual stop, he climbed the steps to street level and paused, acting like he was looking for something. Spying the small café on the corner of the street, he hurried across the intersection between traffic. He entered the café and took a quick glance around at the patrons. Five tables were being used, two pairs of young people and an old man reading a paper, two local constables and a large woman talking loudly on a mobile phone. He walked up to the counter and looked into the mirror above the clerks. He saw that his 'friends' were still behind him, now sitting at an outside table. Not trying to hide themselves today, he thought.

"How can I help you?" said the clerk, dressed in gothic black clothing and sporting a few piercings.

"One cappuccino, large," he replied. It was the standard order he had used here for the last couple of weeks. He had studied this café and had come to it at the same time for weeks.

"Three euros," was the bored reply.

Klaus opened his wallet and pulled out a five-euro note. As usual, the clerk took the note and placed it in the register, turned around and proceeded to make the cappuccino. After placing it in front of him, she reached in and got his change.

"Here is your change," she said, looking at the next customer in line behind him.

"I'm sorry miss," Klaus said sternly, "I gave you a twenty-euro note," as he pointed to the two euro change on the counter. The young clerk look back at him with a pissed off look, one that she had perfected throughout her time in the industry.

"You gave me a five-euro note, sir," she stated the 'sir' with emphasis.

"Young lady, I most certainly did not give you a five note and this is not the first time you have tried this with me," he said in an authoritative voice.

"Listen old man, I might be young, but I'm not stupid. I study mathematics at the university. You gave me a five-euro note and I have never shortchanged you or anyone else. My father owns this café."

Klaus leaned forward over the counter toward the clerk, "I demand to talk to your father then. You are a stealing little tramp and I demand my change back." The clerk closed her eyes and shook her head, then refocused on the irate customer.

"Take your beverage and change and leave NOW!" she screamed.

Klaus acted enraged. He turned to look at the large woman who was describing the incident to whomever she was speaking with on her phone. Klaus's tirade then started on the large woman, "Listen you fat pig," Klaus's face was flushed now and he started approaching the woman, "Can't mind your own fucking business, huh?" He shoved a chair in front of him to the side. The woman began a high-pitched explanation to the caller as she looked around frantically for some sort of support and focused on the two police officers. The two officers watching the event finally got up from their peaceful break and confronted Klaus.

"Calm down sir," one said, raising one of his palms toward Klaus.

Klaus, now in a frenzy, swatted towards the officer's hand. "Fuck off!" Klaus yelled at the policeman.

"That's it sir. Now you have gone a bit too far." The officer grabbed Klaus and swiftly swung Klaus's arm around to his back and clamped handcuffs tightly on and then quickly manacled the other hand.

Outside, the two agents sat mesmerized at the goings-on, powerless to stop their subject. The male agent lifted his sleeve to speak into a microphone and report the incident, but stopped momentarily as Klaus was escorted out and into a police car parked at the corner. As the car drove away, Klaus looked back at the agents and smiled.

"Hey Max, did you have to put them on so tight?" Klaus said laughingly.

Max turned around and said with big grin, "It was Martha's idea, Klaus. I think that large woman wants to experiment with you."

The three laughed as they headed out of Düsseldorf.

CHAPTER NINETEEN

The screen flickered a couple of times before becoming sharp. A large grid overlaid a photo of a large land mass. Jack leaned in closer to look at the monitor.

"Are you telling me this whole area was affected?" he pointed to a four square mile grid area.

"According to these satellite photos and ground reports it covered about two square miles, with the epicenter at the villa where we sent our team," Ted replied dumbfounded. He continued, "Casualties are very high. Our own team was vaporized in the firestorm. Reports from the Brazilian army state that there are over five thousand dead and there was damage to seventy percent of the dwellings in the area. Some parts of the town are still burning as the firestorm leaped over a block or two and started another row of apartments ablaze."

Jack turned around on the ball of his right foot and stared right at Fritz. "Well Dr. Rhinesfalt, what happened and why?" Jack said crossing his arms.

Fritz in his now ever-present annoying, at least to Jack, laissez faire tone, "Gentlemen, the test was a success."

"A success!" Ted yelled, "Five thousand dead a success!"

Jack raised his right hand to Ted to calm him down and looked at Fritz, "Keep going."

Fritz looked back from one to the other, relishing in the tension he had caused.

"Yes, five thousand souls extinguished. A small miscalculation was the contributing factor."

"Miscalculation?" Ted screamed.

"Ted, shut the fuck up. I am trying to find out what happened," Jack spat at him.

"Yes, a misplaced decimal point seemed to widen the SAT beam area by a thousand times. Quite effective really. Take a look at the photos."

Jack looked at the man and wondered, what have I unleashed?

"So you're saying that the whole area was engulfed in the SAT beam, not just the villa?"

"Precisely. Because of the negative dream energy we beamed down to the town, it would have been hard not to be affected if you were sleeping at the time. The cumulative effect of all the negative dream energy accelerated the formation of the negative dreamhub, further intensifying the entire process," Fritz explained calmly.

"Jack," Ted looked at him with pleading eyes, "there have been sporadic reports all over the globe of dozens of other people dying in their sleep while their homes burn. All unrelated according to the news service. What the hell is going on?"

Jack, still with his arms crossed, "Fritz?" now using his first name.

"It would seem that the negative dreamhub we created attracted dreamlines externally. What I mean by externally is that the energy of the negative dreamhub or the nightmare I have created grew to an unusual strength I have not seen to date. Since I know that other dreamers are attracted to the energy, as an energy source the negative dreamhub would attract a large amount of dreams. It seems from Ted's reports that the dreamhub has or still is attracting other dreams from around the world. I have suspected this from earlier experiments years ago, but now in this digital age, reporting is instantaneous. A most curious and intriguing happenstance."

"So you are saying that your negative dreamhub can attract dreams from anywhere in the globe? How can that be?" Jack asked suspiciously.

"I have seen or heard of dreams in the local area of my experiments succumbing to the same fate as my subjects. With this in mind, the dreamhub's energy must pull at the dreams that come close to that energy. The more powerful the dreamhub, the more dreamers. It gets stronger and more are attracted. With several thousand in the same dreamhub, the energy would be enormous, pulling dreamers from anywhere," Fritz stopped with a look of reverence on his face.

"Dreamhubs, lines, this is all in your synopsis report

here?" Jack looked down at a thin folio beside him.

"Yes, all explained. Gentleman, we have created a very powerful tool. A tool that Mein Führer would have salivated to have in his possession."

Both Jack and Ted slowly glanced at each other with unspoken words of 'Oh shit!' between them.

CHAPTER TWENTY

Tony hurried into Peter's lab and headed straight for a computer terminal. Tony's cell phone had chirped, minutes ago, informing him that an e-mail had arrived in his Encryptnow account. Logging into the site, he smiled when he realized that it was Klaus. It had been over a week since his last message, and Tony was wondering if he would be contacted again.

Peter wandered over, stuffing a Montreal smoked meat sandwich into his mouth.

"What's up?" he asked as a piece of meat fell to the floor. Nancy looked over from her workstation with a look of disgust, and then went back to work.

Tony looked up to answer and then touched his chin. Peter wiped some mayo off with the back of his hand, "Sorry," swallowing, "Anything new?"

"Yes. Klaus has just e-mailed me again."

That got the attention of both Nancy and Peter. He continued, "Looks like he was being followed by his own company so he had to arrange his own arrest to get away."

Nancy raised an eyebrow.

"He is in hiding with friends in Zurich now, but he needs to speak with me face to face."

"So we are off to Zurich," Peter started, but Tony kept going.

"He says that I need to get a VOIPMOI account so we can have an encrypted voice communication through the net," Tony commented with a hint of skepticism in his voice.

"VOIPMOI?" Peter questioned.

"I use it all the time." Nancy responded. "It's like a telephone but on the Internet and the calls can't be eavesdropped. I call my grandmother in Australia all the time with it for fun."

"Like the government wants to eavesdrop on your Grandmother's brownie recipe," Peter said sarcastically.

"I would have you know," Nancy snapped quickly, "that her 'magic' brownies are infamous in Hollywood."

Peter, just about to take another bite, glanced sidewise at Tony with a 'Whoa' expression.

Nancy got up with a smug expression laughing to herself and went to Tony's computer. Within two minutes she had the program set up and ready for entry of a new account.

"Ok, all I need is Klaus's VOIPMOI name," she looked at Tony's e-mail and saw the name Klaus had typed. Nancy entered in his contact name and a window popped up stating that Klaus was online.

Tony and Peter jumped when a digital phone ring came

across the computer's external speakers. A window opened asking them if they wanted to accept the call. Nancy looked at Tony, he shrugged his shoulders and she clicked the green phone button.

"Tony, Hello, Tony....are you there?"

"That's Klaus!" Tony exclaimed.

"Of course it's me, who else would it be?" Klaus answered back.

Both Tony and Peter looked at Nancy perplexed.

"Boys, this computer has a built-in microphone in the monitor. All you have to do is talk and Klaus can hear you. It's just like a phone, right Klaus?" she said with a smile on her face.

"Yes, correct to the nice sounding voice there."

Tony shook his head and started up, "Klaus, looks like you had a busy week?"

"My friend, the week is not over," Klaus went on to explain what had transpired over the last few days. Klaus spoke for ten minutes and a stunned silence filled the room.

"Are you safe now?" asked Nancy in a concerned voice.

"I am with close friends hidden away. I want to have time to verify some information that I gathered and I am not happy to tell you that Fritz's experiments have had very destructive results," Klaus outlined the latest test and the firestorm that resulted. Looks of disbelief and shock were shared around the room.

"I saw some report about a town burned to the ground. That was Fritz?" Tony inquired.

"Afraid so, but it gets worse. I have been gathering reports from all over the globe of sporadic deaths in sleep. People burnt to death in their beds, houses seemingly burning down for no reason."

Peter jumped in, "Fritz's dreamhub seems to have a mind of its own. Looks like it is attracting other dreamers, like we experienced with our control group."

"So his artificial nightmare," Tony replied, "turns into one of these dreamhubs."

Peter continued, "Looks like it. I presume that since it caused so many deaths it got out of control. Growing larger and larger, pulling more dreamlines into the hub from all parts of the globe. So that means that these hubs are not local in nature. They can affect dreams worldwide."

"My god," Nancy joined in, "no one should have that type of power."

Klaus had remained silent until now, "From my sources, Fritz intentionally widened the area to be affected when the beam went on. Zicon could have one of the most deadly weapons ever conceived on their hands."

"Klaus," Tony moved close to the monitor, "how many people know about this in your opinion?"

"It has been very well contained. Jack, the CEO of Zicon, has CSU agents doing security, so other than one or two top executives at Zicon and support staff, we are the only other ones."

"Not even the government or military?"

"Not that I can see. Jack would not want this to be known. Its worth is in its secrecy right now. Zicon could command billions for this technology from a number of local and international factions or governments."

"Have you heard of any other experiments coming up?" Peter queried.

"Not so far, but I certainly believe that they will try again or begin demonstrations to sell to potential bidders."

Tony looked over at Peter and said, "No one knows about this. Zicon knows that Klaus knows and I am sure they know that you have been experimenting yourself."

Nancy shifted from one foot to another with her arms crossed and said, "So you are trying to say we are in danger and that we are the only ones that might, big emphasis on might, be the only ones to save the world?"

Tony swiveled his chair around and smiled, drawling in an even thicker Southern accent, "Yes Ma'am, that seems to be the case."

Nancy rolled her eyes and looked straight at Peter and said, "I want a raise!"

A small icon popped up on a monitor and it took Ivan a few minutes to notice it since he had twelve other programs running. Without thinking, he clicked it in passing as he was going back to his other tasks. As soon as the icon was clicked, a preprogrammed set of events happened. First, the program had detected that one of many e-mail addresses being tracked had accessed an encrypted e-mail or VOIP (voice over Internet protocol) service. Second, that the program had established a crack (a hacker's way to access and decode a program) to intercept the transmission. Now, normally this type of crack was not conceivable as it dealt with almost unbreakable 128-bit encryption and the average hacker did not have the resources to attack this. Ivan, though, had access to the full resources of Zicon, including three supercomputers, the top dog of computing ever devised. And if that was not enough, Ivan had written a zombie Trojan script which, in layman terms, meant that he could run any program he wanted on all the networked computers in the whole Zicon corporation, over 100,000 computers. Each computer was daisy-chained without the computer operator's knowledge to work on a portion of the problem at hand. The daisy-chained computers now became the equivalent of 100 supercomputers. Having all these computing resources allowed Ivan to use the easiest but most lengthy method to break the encryption: the brute force method. Simply put, the computers would use every conceivable combination of the encryption key possible in a systematic search.

Time flew by as the numbers were crunched throughout the night by the network of computers performing a silent dance of bits and bytes. Several hours later, at four in the morning, another icon appeared and did its audible chirp. Ivan raised his head from the desk, the imprint of the corner of a keyboard embedded in his forehead. He instinctively clicked the icon. Immediately, an audio playback program opened and started playing. Ivan sat there still half asleep but woke up quickly at the mention of Tony, Klaus and then Fritz. Immediately, he re-routed the audio file to a compression program and then sent the newly encrypted audio file to Ted's SAT phone.

He shook his head, still groggy, and typed madly, sending another program over the Internet for another stealthy search.

CHAPTER TWENTY-ONE

Eyes open, at least I think they just opened. Blackness surrounds me, like being in the vacuum of space. Am I alive? Am I dead? I am thinking, so I must be alive in some form. Think, yes think. Where was I? What was I doing? How did I get here?

"Hello?" I yell. No sound. Did I yell out? I raise my hand to my face, I see nothing. Is it really there? I must be in a chamber totally cut off. What is that? A pinpoint of light to my left.

"Hello? Hello!" I yell again.

Again no reply, no sound. The light grows larger. No sound. The light continues to grow larger like it is heading my way. My way? Movement then, but it is taking its time to get to me. How large is this chamber? It is coming faster now. More than just a light. A beam of light fading to nothing in the distance. It is coming close to me. I reach out to the light which is very near now, and fast. So fast. Still trying to get closer, but I suddenly start being pushed away. I try desperately to reach the light, but it shoots by pushing me away like a balloon in the wind. I tumble over and over until I see another light beam closing in from another direction. I start to reach out, but feel that I am being pulled in this time.

Closer, I approach…it is going to pass me by again. I am so close. It has passed me again. Whoa…it's got me! I have been grabbed by it. I am now traveling beside this beam of light. It feels like I have never gone this fast before. I see other beams of light now crossing this expanse. I am definitely not in a chamber. How did I get here? The beam of light is right beside me and I reach over to touch it. Heat, burning, I pull away. No pain. I try again. Heat and burning, but I do not pull away. I am in a chair burning. Yes, I remember now.

I see images from above the earth, mountains that are snow-capped. Snow, I have never touched real snow. I am looking through a window. This must be a plane. I take my hand away from the beam of light and the images are gone. I am back to the blackness and weaving lines of light.

These beams. Where are they going? Where is this one taking me? I now see something different . A large light, very strong light. I feel my beam being pulled towards it. I can see other beams from all over turning towards it. We are closer now. I see the large light turning like a windmill, pulsing as beams of light intersect it. We are going towards it faster. I remember about black holes. Is this one? Faster, I force my eyes open to see when I join it. No fear, only curiosity.

My beam is almost there…almost…I find myself on a large balcony overlooking a beautiful sprawling city.

.

Architecture from all the ages of time clutter the skyline, along with huge tracts of wheat fields and forests. The ambient air temperature is perfect, no cold, no heat. I turn around to see the rest of the balcony and right there, behind me, is a being. I look up to the beautiful being.

"Who are you?" it asks in a sensual voice. Sound, I hear sound.

"My name is Manuel," I reply, my memories flood back. "Yes, I am Manuel."

Luis had contacted his cousin Ernesto, a captain in the Costa Rican police force for the southwestern region. Ernesto, usually dealing with petty crimes on tourists in the town of Quepos, was very concerned. For one thing, Luis never asked favors of Ernesto, even though Ernesto had offered many times. Many times to get a kickback, Luis had thought often as his teak tree plantation business grew. Kickbacks for certain concessions from local officials. Luis and Manuel's business had grown steadily without the meddling of bureaucrats.

Ernesto had also played chess against Manuel. He knew him well. So, once Ernesto got the call from Luis, he responded immediately, a response quite in defiance of the slow pace which is the Central American normal speed. He put out an all-points bulletin on the blue car, with detailed descriptions of the two occupants based on the boy's recollection.

A radio car passing Parritta towards Quepos had seen a blue car speeding out of the Palo Seco road back toward

Jaco. When the radio call went out about twenty minutes later, an officer radioed in that he had seen it. Another police car, halfway from Jaco, heard the report as well and reported that he was heading straight for it on the same road. However, a half an hour later, the police car entered Parritta and radioed in that it had not passed the vehicle. Ernesto then concluded that the blue car had turned off between Parritta and half way to Jaco. Several private roads to beach properties came off the highway. Many unsavory characters hid along that stretch. Good practice for his SIG tactical squad, very good practice, he thought.

CHAPTER TWENTY-TWO

Ivan was pleased with himself. His little hitchhiker script had worked. Calling up another self-written script, he typed in a command. Within seconds, two bits of information came across his screen, IP addresses and approximate locations. Ivan opened another cola and raised it in self-congratulations. He had outsmarted his opponents, knowing that they had a leak at Zicon. Ivan had imbedded a small, very small program or Trojan, as the tech world called it, into a digital picture. No one would be able to detect it as it was actually part of the digital file. Actually, it was a pixel in the picture. It would be extremely hard, almost impossible, to detect among the millions of pixels in one picture. It didn't take long for the digital file to be uploaded. Someone had hacked into the Zicon main server, this time allowed by Ivan, and the data was taken out, but to where? This is where the hitchhiker came to life. As soon as the file was saved on the hacker's hard drive, the program would self-execute and then worm itself into the computer system files to find out its IP address. The fun part, at least to Ivan, was that no matter what encryption or security procedures hid the transfer or protected the file, it had to be opened on a computer somewhere. When it did, the hitch-hiker awoke. Smiling to himself, Ivan picked up the phone and dialed.

"Sir, I've got two hits for you on my hitchhiker," he said.

"Do tell," replied Ted.

"One in Zurich, and of all places Boston, Massachusetts."

"Boston, huh? Do you have more detailed locations?"

"I'll have that within minutes and will encrypt that to your phone."

"I'll buy you some shares in that cola you drink for this one."

"I'll hold you to that, out."

Ivan leaned back in his chair and took a long swallow of his cola. Minutes later Ted had the information he needed.

"Jack," Ted started on his cell, "we have a location on Klaus and it looks like he has passed the info onto Peter's group in Boston."

"Do you have a location on them?"

"Looks like the info went to their lab," Ted surmised.

"I need home locations for the two in Boston, Ted. We need to take care of this right now. I will handle Herr Klaus from here," Jack said.

"Handle permanently?"

"Yes, god damn it Ted. This is too large to have this group meddling in."

"I'll find them Jack," Ted's phone went to a dial tone after the click.

"What an asshole," Ted muttered to himself.

Ted's CSU agents, using the information from Ivan, had soon located both Nancy and Peter's homes. With limited manpower in Boston, Ted decided to take care of the easier target first. The CSU team sat in a City Engineering van located at the entrance of an alley at the target's building. They had quickly set up a miniature surveillance camera across the street, disguised as a discarded package of smokes, to keep an eye on the target's windows. The apartment lights were on and the target had previously been seen parking in the garage. Ted wanted a clean operation, but time was a factor. It would have be a quick in and out with minimal exposure. As Ted sat in his jet seat flying over the Gulf of Mexico, a signal came in telling him that the CSU team was in place and ready to commence. Ted typed in the order to the team leader: 'Go', and pressed Send on the phone. The team sat and waited, watching the monitor of the hidden camera's output until the lights went out in the apartment.

Ted sat forward and started scanning the three video screens. They were tied in to movie-cams attached to the three agent's helmets. It was like watching a video game. Ted saw the team depart from a van located in an alley and enter the building from a side door close by.

Fritz was anxious to proceed with the next phase of

surgically sending his death beam to earth to affect an individual somewhere on the planet. He smirked at the term 'death beam' which was being used by the agents stationed at the compound. Jack had told him his target was in Zurich and he had looked up the location data at the central control panel in the research building. All parameters entered, Fritz looked at one of the clocks that annoyingly ticked all day long. Two o'clock in the morning, time to set things in motion.

The CSU team had successfully reached the correct floor from the side stairwell. Luckily, at this early hour, no one was stirring. The building was quiet. Only the hum of the boiler below permeated in the air. The team leader cracked open the fire door and looked down the hallway. Bare whitewashed walls and worn carpets. No sign of life. They proceeded down to the apartment of their target: 4C. The lead agent carefully and masterfully inserted a lock-picking device, feeling for the lock disengaging mechanism. The other two agents behind him were tense, scanning the area in both directions; silenced pistols in hand. The lock made a quiet click and very slowly the door was opened. They entered the apartment, closed the door behind them and moved along the wall acclimatizing themselves to their new environment. Streetlight filtered through partially closed blinds throwing a lightened pattern across the living room. Simple furniture was centrally located facing a small fireplace. No obstructive tables or knick-knacks blocked entrance to that room. According to the layout plans Ivan had located with another program and had downloaded to their laptop, they were aware that the bedroom was to the left of the living room. With a hand signal, the lead agent gestured one of them to stay at the front door to keep their escape covered. The other agent was to go through the other rooms, just in case there was an unknown occupant present.

Making sure he saw his agent heading towards the kitchen, the lead agent approached the bedroom. At the entrance, he mentally rehearsed the scenario. He was to quickly subdue the target and then inject a non-traceable lethal mixture that he surmised Zicon had manufactured. This would leave the target unconscious, to die slowly over the next ten minutes. His mental plan set, he quickly entered the bedroom and went straight toward the bed only to find the bed sheets were pulled back over an empty bed.

He clicked on his radio mike, "Target not here." Immediately the second agent replied, "Dwelling secure," meaning no individuals were present in the area that he had swept. The third agent stationed at the entrance reported, "Entrance still secure."

"Abort, abort," was the reply from the lead agent.

Nancy walked down towards her favorite late night haunt, the sound of her footsteps echoing between the quiet buildings. Being a night owl, she was used to the street and the characters that roamed like her at that hour. She welcomed the adventure quite often during the week. She walked up to the glass-paned door, smiling as she thought of the warm cinnamon buns inside the bakery.

The SAT beam had now saturated the dwelling for over five minutes. Usually, it automatically shut off after two minutes. Fritz walked over to the window and looked out over his compound. Soon, he thought, soon.

At the end of the hallway, sounds of typing permeated through the closed wooden door. The old clock's small airplane-shaped minute hand swept by twelve again, making it five past two. The typing stopped momentarily as outside the window on the street a couple stopped and stared toward the right. They both started pointing and one of them pulled out a cell phone and began yelling into it. Taking off the loud headphones, Peter now could hear the horrible sounds coming down the hallway from behind him. Quickly opening the door, he saw flames and smoke pouring from the other bedroom's slightly opened door down the hall.

"Tony!" Peter screamed as he ran towards the flaming room. The hallway ceiling was alight with flames as the fire spread quickly. Peter's mind was reeling; his self-preservation fighting the urge he knew would get him killed. The fire was too intense, almost leaping ahead of him, searching a way to cut off his escape. Peter hurried back to his room slamming the home office door behind him and grabbed the only thing of value in his life, his laptop. Luckily he lived in an old building. He managed to climb out of the open office window to the metal fire escape that he had cursed each weekend, as it had seemed to be the party stairway to a suite above him at all hours of the night. As he descended the iron rung fire escape ladder, tears soaked his shirt not only from the smoke, but also from the loss of his good friend.

Ever so slightly, the focus of the SAT beam moved according to the programming many miles above.

Nancy casually strolled down the sidewalk thinking of nothing. Her mind was on neutral, oblivious to her surroundings while enjoying the last bites of her cinnamon bun. She came to a street corner and began to walk into the street when a fire engine raced by, lights and sirens blaring.

Jesus, she thought as she hopped back onto the sidewalk, Wakey, wakey Miss Nancy.

The fire truck had now turned the corner and out of her sight, but she heard it slow down and stop, the sirens now winding down. A horrible feeling twisted in the pit of her stomach, and it was definitely not from the bun. She paused for a second then ran towards the location of the emergency lights now reflecting a kaleidoscope of colors on the apartment buildings around the corner. Upon reaching the intersection, she saw a different type of light reflecting in glass- paned storefronts located on the ground level of the buildings now in front of her. Nancy fell to her knees in utter shock as she witnessed her four-story apartment building engulfed in flames.

CHAPTER TWENTY-THREE

He was still in a happy little dream, in the nose of a glider high above a lush green valley. The only sound was the wind whistling past the fuselage. Tony looked around and saw that he was the only occupant. The glider was flying by itself. He marveled at the sleekness and fragility of the craft as he took in the 15-meter wingspan stretching out from the tube-like fuselage. Tony was mesmerized at the beauty of the valley below, an endless jungle of some sort stretched out to the horizon.

Suddenly, the glider dove toward the ground. Tony's vision began tunneling because of the g-force that was pushing against him. Still falling, he noticed that the ground never came closer. Looking to the left, Tony saw many fuzzy colored lines that seemed to be following the glider. At first, his vision was distorted like a person high on some hallucinogenic. As he still headed downward, all he saw were smoothed edged shapes. The glider began to spin to the left. His vision now became sharp as a tack as the ground suddenly came screaming toward him. His altimeter spun downward surreally and within seconds the nose of the glider began drilling itself through the top foliage of the jungle canopy below by spinning in a counter-clockwise motion.

Leaves were torn away, branches snapped taking spider monkeys to the jungle floor. The sound was horrendous as the glider sliced through the trees. Snapping sounds, the chorus of screeching animals and birds filled the air as they were all now in flight, running away from the intruder in their midst. Tony hung on inside the glider which was still intact, even as it hit the jungle floor still spinning.

Decomposing ferns and topsoil sprayed upon impact, but the glider still spun drilling into the ground. The wings snapped off as they came in contact with the ground, now making the fuselage a cylindrical drill that sped up with less drag. Tony was beyond dizzy. His vision was just snapshots of a fast-forwarding film. Bracing himself with his arms and feet to the inside of the fuselage, he tried to hang on to normalcy. It never came as the glider began to drill further into the earth, passing crushed rocks and boulders. Nothing stopped the indestructible glider. It now passed through the earth's mantel, the top crust protecting the earth. Tony sensed the temperature change as the glider, now just a driller, traveled faster and deeper. Sweat started forming on his body and the windows of the craft steamed up with condensation. His vision was now back to normal. He was one with the driller, like an astronaut spinning in his capsule. Tony saw a yellow glow far way as the cabin became hotter and hotter. The air quickly became stale to the point where it was almost too hot to breath. Tony was more curious than worried, as he had had indescribable nightmares before.

A piece of smoldering plastic fell on his bare leg instigating the first hint of pain. He patted it away only to feel his back beginning to sink into the melting seat. A strong willed man, Tony fought not to cry out, but the whole cabin began to glow from the heat. Tony looked out and saw an orange flowing mass. Molten lava registered in his brain as he now knew he was drilling to the center of the earth. He ground his teeth, knowing that this was not your garden-variety nightmare. Fritz had gotten to him.

Tony kept his casual smile as his hair ignited and his skin began to melt, becoming one with the vessel shooting towards the earth's core. Completely enveloped in a molten orange environment, Tony was relieved when suddenly darkness, light beams and a sense of gravity became points of reference. I am here, he thought, I am actually in the dreamweave.

Tony scanned his environment. Off to the side in a large Renaissance ballroom, Tony studied the workmanship of the valances near the ceiling. Real or not, he pondered and smirked to himself as he watched a graceful formal dance in progress. The participants were flowing from one movement to another. The modern band playing off to the side was surreal.

Ok, he thought, I have left all reality behind.

"Yes you have," a voice behind him replied.

Tony turned around curiously at the voice. You can

read my mind? he thought.

"Only what is meant to be heard," was the verbal reply.

"Intriguing," said Tony.

He studied the new arrival with interest. Dressed in a stunning renaissance gown, its torso was human, or as much as it could be described, floating on a shimmering constantly moving mass that never touched the floor.

"No questions?" it asked.

Tony took a moment and checked out the being from head to whatever was below and saw that she had a beauty that was indescribable. Tony's eyes reflected his admiration and the being smiled immediately.

"I will not read your mind if you wish," it said as it continued to smile.

"That I would appreciate," Tony said, trying to keep improper thoughts out of his head. What a looker, well half of her at least, he thought freely. What is it? What do I call this being? Tony could not come up with a name to this beauty, so he just named it, "the Being". The Being shifted slightly to the right and changed color below the waist.

Tony started, "I understand that I am in the dreamweave inside a dreamhub. I presume that I have either died or I am in a prolonged dream?"

"Curious that you use the terms dreamweave and dreamhub. Very appropriate for the environment here. Yes, you have died."

Tony swallowed hard as anxiety flushed through his system, but he still listened.

"As have all who are *Here*," She waved her hand slowly across the room.

"Yourself included?"

"Consider me the host," she retorted, "a limited guide."

"So there are other such places to visit?" Tony started his scientific investigation, trying to gain the most information he could gather, especially since it, the Being, appeared willing to talk.

"I only know of *Here* and how you arrive," it said as the colors changed constantly beneath her.

"The beams of light," Tony said more as a fact than a question.

"Yes, all travel by beams to arrive to *Here*."

"This is a stopping area then, before traveling on?" He stopped to look around the room, again letting the fantasy become somewhat real.

"This is the only place," she replied with a look of satisfaction on her ruby lips.

Tony, pausing for a moment, dissected the information and pondered. This entity only knows of this place and the method we get here. Interesting.

Tony tried another angle, "Is this all that there is, the ballroom?"

The Being floated out of a large doorway and then toward a balcony. Tony followed and then stood in awe at the vision presented. The vista from the balcony pointed to a horizon many miles away.

"This is *Here*," she smiled, then frowned quickly, "but

it becomes smaller."

"Smaller?" Tony replied quickly.

"Yes, *Here* was once endless. All have their own ways to express it within," she waved her arm back toward the ballroom.

Tony now had too many questions. He had to quickly prioritize his list. Tony started slowly, "So this, *Here*, as you call it, was larger. Why and when did it become smaller?" He hoped that the questioning wouldn't scare her away.

The Being turned back toward Tony and answered, "When things were brighter."

Great, Tony thought, didn't think it would be easy. "Brighter?" he said.

"Yes," she smiled. "*Here* was much brighter, with much more color. It is now dull."

Tony did not understand. How much more color could exist in such a place? It looked colorful enough to him.

The Being carried on, "Once, the sky was emerald in color. Beings like yourself added color. Lately, the sky has become lackluster."

Tony did not try to interpret this. He kept on questioning, "How long ago was this?"

She tilted her head sideways, "I have been asked about this before, a reference to time. I know no such thing, but can offer the only way you beings have to measure time."

Tony stood waiting as the Being floated back towards the inside of the ballroom. Tony followed her, still mesmerized by her form of movement.

"Dullness began when this type of clothing

appeared."

Tony followed her outstretched arm to where it pointed. Standing in the corner were three women dressed in beautiful formal gowns talking to a man in full black attire. The man turned toward one of the women and coming into view was an armband with a swastika.

CHAPTER TWENTY-FOUR

If you were looking at an overhead view of the city, you would have seen two cabs swerving and turning from different points both racing toward the campus. Peter knew it was chancy to go to the lab, but vital files were on his hard drive. With his cell phone out, Peter speed-dialed Nancy's number and immediately got her voice-mail.

Damn it, he thought, she's on the phone at this time of the night?

Nancy swore under her breath, "Fucking voice-mail!" and hit redial immediately yelling a quick message to Peter when his greeting had ended.

Peter's cell phone chirped telling him that a message had just been received. Keying in his password, his ear was blasted by Nancy's screaming voice.

"Peter, they burned down my building! I am on the way to the lab, please call me!" The sound didn't stop as she must have not ended the call correctly. "I said take the next right damn it". Peter heard the squealing of tires as the cab must have taken a sharp corner. "Run the red…" The call ended.

Peter was about to hit redial when his phone vibrated and he answered it.

"Peter! Oh my god, I am so scared!" she said.

"Nancy, are you OK?"

Nancy just went off for the next two minutes telling him detail after detail. He sat back and started formulating a plan while passively listening.

By the time she took a breath he started, "Nancy, OK. I am also five minutes from the lab and I can't explain what is happening until we meet. I will see you soon." Peter hung up.

Nancy pulled the phone from her ear and stared at it in a state of shock. "Well piss on you," she said as she brutally pressed the End button.

Peter's cab came to a rolling stop in front of the building, and while paying the driver, another cab arrived in the roundabout driveway. Nancy did not even wait for the cab to stop, jumping out and throwing money at the driver. She ran toward Peter as he stepped out of his cab and from out of nowhere Nancy's palm struck him right across his cheek.

"Don't you ever hang up on me again you bastard," she screamed.

Peter, by reflex, grabbed her wrist, pulled her closer and in a very strong, quiet, soothing voice said, "Tony's dead."

The fire in Nancy's eyes immediately extinguished. It was a good thing Peter still held on to her wrist as she simply crumbled. Peter brought around his other arm and cradled her as she wept. He held her tight. As the stillness of the night enveloped both of them, the last cab rounded the corner. Peter held Nancy closely and gave her some time then explained what had happened at his place.

They were sitting on the curb, Nancy still holding Peter's hands sniffling. With the hurt in her eyes, he could tell that she had thought Tony was special. Her eyes changed slowly at first and then quickly back to the fire he had previously seen. She was pissed.

Peter got up and said, "We have to be quick and get out of here." Nancy looked up and nodded.

Inside the lab, Nancy worked quickly on Tony's computer accessing the VOIPMOI program, hoping Klaus was online. Peter was frantically downloading data and Tony's dreamweave program onto his laptop, then onto his mp3 for a backup. Luckily he had that on his belt loop when he had fled. The mp3, although mainly a music player, was actually an 80 GB hard drive that had more than enough memory to handle the information he was backing up.

Better to have two backups of the data, he thought.

Nancy started, "Klaus….Klaus this is Nancy in Boston."

Klaus came through the speakers, "You sound stressed, is everything OK?"

Nancy, back to the levelheaded assistant, chronologically went through the order of events in the last two hours. Klaus asked a couple of minor questions and stifled an outburst at the news of Tony.

Klaus finally broke in, "You two are in extreme

danger."

"No shit!" was Nancy's response.

Peter rolled his eyes at her response as Klaus continued on, "You both need to get to Zurich immediately. Tell no one. It may take longer to be safe, so fly through Canada then to Amsterdam and take a train to Zurich from there. Watch your back because Zicon's agents are damn well looking for you."

Nancy looked up from the screen to Peter with a look of 'can we do this'?

Peter nodded his head agreeing and smirked, "My budget is going to be screwed this month."

CHAPTER TWENTY-FIVE

Klaus had left instructions on how to reach him. He did not know at the time if he would stay put or not. Hearing about Tony certainly had him wondering. It looked like anyone associated with the research would be eliminated. Although he felt he was in a reasonably secure place, it lacked the equipment or room needed to continue Peter's experiments.

He quickly packed his bag and left through the parkade. He had borrowed a car from friends, not wanting to use traceable means to find him. As he exited outside, the parade of streetlights started their dance, slowly flickering as they became alight. He started heading towards Visp, Switzerland, two and a half hours southeast from Zurich. A small city where his old friend and colleague Werner lived and worked. He hadn't talked with him in a few years, but he was a creature of habit and one of those types of friends with whom you could pick up the conversation years later like nothing had happened in between.

Werner lived to work and would chomp at the bit to help out Klaus. Klaus had once saved one of Werner's businesses by using his contacts. Medical innovation was a prosperous and challenging industry but also short-lived if your funding dried up. Klaus had secured private funding that helped Werner turn his business into one of the strongest in the world.

Hitting the power window down, Klaus smelt the cooling night air and smiled to himself. Yes, Werner would be there working away as usual. Klaus accelerated along the highway as a glimmer of hope finally came to him.

Ted had been anxiously waiting for the reports from Boston. Finally an encrypted test message came across his SAT phone.

SUBJ: Target Status

Both targets NOT eliminated. First target not present in dwelling. As Team prepared for second target, first target's apartment building went up in flames. At arrival of second target, second target's building also in flames. Eye witness reports of second target escaping blaze by fire escape and fleeing scene by cab. Now on route to third location.

END TEXT TRANSMISSION

Ted was furious. First, he did not have enough men on the ground in Boston. He would have imagined a three-prong attack rather than a game of who's next. Most unprofessional, he thought. His next thoughts were more of shock. Shock at the reports of the fires. Fires in Boston? This had to be Fritz's doing. That old kraut is out of control and is out of his fucking mind, he thought. Ted immediately called Jack, but the line came up with that annoying, 'All circuits are busy' crap and the fast beeping shrill. Ted winced as he pulled the phone from his ear and then hit the text message button. He rapidly typed a quick synopsis of the recent events to Jack. After he pressed the Send button, he went back to finding out the status in Boston. Fritz was Jack's problem. It was his pet project and he would wait for the next orders.

The van took the last turn at breakneck speed and sped up the circular driveway. The agents spilled out of the back. Stealth was not an issue anymore as the order had come down to just get the job done. The four-man team rushed the front door of the university lab's entrance. Smashing through the glass doorway they fanned out across the now unoccupied reception area. Security was lax at this time of night. The team leapfrogged down the hallway toward Peter's lab. They had all the schematics of the building sent to them by Ivan while they were on route. They wasted no time once they got to the lab's door. One member busted the door with a small battering ram, and then the others rushed in. Within ten seconds, the 'all clear' confirmations had been voiced. Peter and Nancy had already left. The lead agent got on his phone and called Ivan, "Our two have left the lab already. Check the cab companies."

Ivan was already on it as soon as he heard the word 'left'. Hacking into the dispatch logs of the major cab companies in Boston took mere minutes for the talented hack.

"Child's play," he said out loud to himself. "Ok," speaking to the agent, "I have a yellow cab number 2471 leaving the lab ten minutes ago. Looks like it dropped them off already at the corner of Tremont and Ruggles street."

"What's there?" was the reply.

Ivan pulled up an Internet map site quickly, "Well, looks like it is the Boston Police Headquarters."

"What!" was the agent's exclamation as he pressed the End button and then speed dialed Ted. As soon as he heard the word "Secured" from Ted, the agent updated him quickly.

"Well fuck me," was Ted's response with a big roll of his eyes. "Ok, go dark for now," and ended his conversation. The agents and van disappeared within a minute to go back on stand by mode.

Other than a laptop bag and Nancy's purse, the two traveled light. Everything else was gone. They were out of the lab within minutes of talking to Klaus, grabbing a cab and heading downtown. The air in the cab was charged from the nervous energy of the two sitting in the back seat. Peter was particularly nervous as he had this nagging suspicion that they had just narrowly escaped from the lab. He felt like he was being watched, even from afar. He had told the cab driver to go downtown for now but then he got an idea. He leaned over to the driver and said, "Take us to the police headquarters."

"What!" Nancy yelled out, "I thought we were going...," an elbow jabbed her ribs cutting off the location before she blurted it out. Also Peter gave her a sidewise 'shut the hell up' look and then smirked. She sat back and rubbed her sore side. When they got to Police Headquarters they waited for the cab to leave and then Peter flagged another. Nancy was perplexed but got in anyway. Once inside, Peter pushed forty bucks through the window and said, "Train station. No meter and don't call it in."

"No problem bud," said the driver and then sped away. Peter relaxed into the seat feeling good that he might have outsmarted whoever was after them.

As they arrived at the station they scurried out of the cab and ran up to the ticket window in time to find out that an express train to Montreal was just about to leave. Being last minute, all they could secure on the train was a first class, private cabin sleeping two. Peter winced at the price he paid in cash. Money was going to be a problem quickly. They had both taken out what they could from the campus ATM just inside the reception area. Credit cards were out of the question, as everyone knew they could be tracked very easily. They literally boarded the train as it started moving away from the station. Entering their cabin Peter thought, this is all we get for first class? A slightly larger cabin than most, with a private bathroom and shower. Well, at least they would have privacy. The train had picked up speed and semi-blurred images streamed passed the window. Nancy took one look into the bathroom and just said, "Dibs" closing the door behind her.

Minutes later, Peter turned around at the sound of a door opening. Nancy came through drying her hair and wearing a towel wrapped around her body. She looked up and stopped dead in her tracks.

"What?" she said looking at Peter's gaze.

Peter quickly looked away, "Sorry, Nance," his pet name for her, "it just seems strange seeing you like that."

"Like what?" she smirked, continuing to dry her hair with a thick towel.

"A girl, that's all. Not as my assistant."

Nancy skirted by Peter and sat down on the lower bunk. "Well, this girl is hungry."

Peter returned to the cabin to find Nancy transformed back to his assistant. A twinge of regret flashed through his mind at his last glimpse of her. She had set up the laptop on top of the small fold-down table at the window. The countryside was now flashing by like a blur.

"Breakfast sandwiches are the take de jour," he said as he handed her a bag and placing down two coffees. The next few minutes were filled with the sounds of chewing, lip smacking and normal sounds of a voracious animal devouring its prey. Peter sat back after watching the slaughter of the innocent sandwich.

"Always a delight to see you dine," he said sarcastically. He had seen this many times, knowing that Nancy needed to eat, or watch out. It was well-known around the campus about the unsuspecting humans who had been given verbal and almost physical abuse by Nancy and her hypoglycemic needs.

Nancy did not even respond to the comment, finished her sandwich then got back to work. Placing the remnants in the bag she tossed it to the floor. She then spun the laptop around so Peter could see what she had done.

The laptop screen was broken into two side-by-side panels. The right side a white background with a stream of scrolling text and numbers. The left had a black background with a spiraling brilliant white sphere with tendrils.

"A negative dreamhub," Peter said without expression.

"Correct."

Nancy clicked a button and the dreamhub rotated counter clockwise.

"How…" Peter started when Nancy interrupted.

"I was just getting to that," she rewound the video on the screen, "Last night I e-mailed one of the students that took part in our last experiment." Nancy stopped the rewind and hit play. The dreamhub started back on its turn.

"The kid is a programming genius. All I did was give him some parameters, explained to him our theory on the negative hub and what I wanted visually and he gave me this," Nancy glowed while pointing to the screen.

"Continue," Peter said crossing his arms knowing she was on a roll.

"I just checked my e-mail account. Good call on

getting the cabin with wireless high speed Internet by the way. This kid, Joseph, wrote a program that searches the Internet news feeds and blogs for occurrences of death while sleeping over the last month or two. Using the data that we gathered in our last experiment with our positive dreamhub and then scaling it to what we saw," Nancy took a sip of her coffee, "versus the incoming data from the news feeds, his software compiles it all and gives us a visual representation of the negative hub in a real time format."

Peter looked from Nancy's still-glowing face back to the screen. His mind was flying at super sonic speed now with the information received. "This kid did this in a few hours?" he now sat forward looking at the screen.

"He said it was simple and he only wanted to be involved in the next experiment we did," she smirked.

"I bet he does. Ok, so what was that white line that just flew into the hub?"

"In his e-mail he said that the program actively searches the Internet for reports. When one occurs from the geographical position of the occurrence, a dreamline of the 'dead dreamers,' that is all I could think of calling them, shows itself and flies into the hub causing the hub to grow in size. See, here comes another." Nancy pointed to the screen as more lines started coming into view, circling and then joining the hub.

"Those all came from this quadrant?" Peter pointed.

Nancy played with the laptop's mouse pad and placed the arrow on the bottom right hand screen.

'Boston, Mass' came upon the screen in a small text box.

"This is a playback of last night," she said sullenly. "Tony was one of those."

She looked out the window, watching the blur of trees realizing again that Tony was gone. Peter looked perplexed at the interface of the software, still amazed at the ingenuity of the human mind. To write software so quickly, so easily, he thought. He clicked the mouse pad and requested 'Access Real Time'.

The hub image grew in size when it started again, a swarm of dreamlines circling the larger hub.

"Jesus Nancy, this can't be right!"

Nancy grabbed and took over the mouse from Peter. She pointed it to the source of the now hundreds of lines emerging.

"Zurich, Switzerland," showed in the text box.

"Klaus," was all Nancy said in a low frightened voice.

CHAPTER TWENTY-SIX

Tony looked down from the grand balcony at the cobblestone street below. A myriad of vehicles passed by; an old Model T, a 70's muscle car, an old New York cab and even a horse and carriage. The city, if you could call it that, was in a state of panic. You could feel the edge in the air.

If that is air I'm breathing, if I'm breathing at all! Tony thought. A movement to Tony's right made him look as the Being floated onto the balcony, now garbed in a 1920's flapper outfit. He could not help but stare again at her beauty.

"Have you seen the changes?" she asked with one of the sweetest voices Tony had ever heard.

"Yes, it has changed since the darkness," he said. Tony had learned quite a bit since he had arrived. No one called it day and night as there was no sun or moon, just light and darkness. The concept of time was very surreal. You thought in moments here, not really having a clue of how long it had been since you had arrived.

The Being replied, "The colors are fading."

"Sepia, it is called," Tony said. "A process of color that photographers used, after black and white photography started and before color film."

"This sepia is everywhere and many more have arrived," she said.

Tony had sensed that there were more here now even since he arrived.

"*Here* has reduced in size again. Many streets no longer exist, but they still remain."

"They?" Tony quipped staring out into the city.

"You. The arrivals still remain. You should be gone."

"You mean none of the arrivals have left here since the man with that suit," he pointed to the swastika that was ever present.

"Yes, you have not left. You are supposed to leave, but it seems only a few have."

"Where do we go?" Tony said. He was now catching on to her way of speaking.

"That I do not know. Only that you arrive and then you go."

Tony knew better than to ask how long between coming and going, so he said, "So how many have not gone?"

"When the swastika, as you called it, appeared some do come and go as they should, but a greater number have stayed."

Tony felt an energy wave flow through him.

"Many more have arrived and stayed while *Here* has become smaller."

Tony shuddered at the comment, "Can you do anything

about this?"

"Nothing, to be done, only be," she said as she smiled and floated over the balcony toward the city.

Tony stood there for what seemed like hours and analyzed the situation. He began reviewing the information to himself.

I and or we are all dead, we probably all died in our sleep, dreaming. I know I traveled through the dreamweave before arriving here. I saw brilliant lines, and snippets of dreams when I could touch their lines. At least I know what they are. These poor souls have no clue what they went through. Probably for the best.

OK, so *Here* is maybe another dreamhub? Sure looked like one that we saw in the lab, but things are not right here according to the beautiful Being.

Tony paused and looked up as a brilliantly colorful hot air balloon slowly floated by. Guess some things here are still right after all. *Here*, from all accounts of the architecture, had been around for a millennia or two. Tony had seen a real Roman garden once while walking around.

Another larger energy wave happened again. There is a sense of panic. Tony thought, where? Why? I cannot explain it...Damn! What is there to be panicking about... I'm dead and seem to have lots of time on my hands. The arrivals coming lately reduces *Here's* size quicker.

Tony lifted his hand from the railing and distractedly stroked his chin. No stubble! Now that is interesting, he mused. No time, no growth, no aging, I guess!

Ok, so us, the arrivals show up and then we are supposed

to go somewhere else. God knows where…hmmm…God. Don't even want to think about that, he thought shaking his head. So, if we are all supposed to leave and only a few do, that means something is stopping the normal process, or the arrivals that stay are different.

He was interrupted as another person came up the railing of the large balcony. Tony turned away and continued to himself.

The altered arrivals started around the time of World War II, back in the land of reality. No coincidence that Fritz had started his dream experimentation in the camps around that time. Well then, Fritz really fucked up *Here* for the last sixty years. His negative dreamhubs must have changed the laws of *Here*.

Tony fell to the floor as the balcony shook and he made contact with something. Recovering from the shock, he sat up, shook his head to see what he had hit.

"Big one," was the quote from the fellow Tony had just bumped into.

"Largest yet," Tony replied. The energy waves were getting much stronger.

"The end is near," the fellow replied.

"The end of what is the question?" Tony said flippantly as he got back on his feet and brushed himself off. The other fellow did the same.

"The end of *Here*," he replied quickly.

"You sound like that Being I met."

"Yes, I might at that. She is distressed. She can not do anything since the waves have really gained strength recently."

Tony studied the man, obviously of Latin descent, based on his accent and skin color. He appeared sure of himself. Almost anticipating Tony's question, he started up, "My name is Manuel and I have been here, well not that I know for sure but for quite a while anyway. When I arrived the waves were coming in very low, almost hard to detect, but the last few dozen have been dramatic."

"You have been here a while then and you say it will be the end of *Here*? Can you expand on that?" As an after thought he added, "I am sorry, Tony is my name," extending his hand. Manuel shook his hand.

Manuel smiled and said, "I have had many conversations with what you call the Being and others who are here. I have also sought out some that I had spoken to before but they seem to have vanished."

"The Being mentioned that they, or we, are all supposed to leave."

"Yes. She said this to me as well. I sense that this is a place you come to before you reach your destiny. Everyone I have talked to has died in their sleep as far as they know."

Bingo! was Tony's thought.

"That is what I have deduced. I think that is the appropriate word," Manuel shrugged his shoulders trying to come out with the proper English.

"Yes. Close. Deduced is the proper word," Tony replied thinking this man is intelligent.

"Yes, of course, deduced that they stay here in a sort

of queue, waiting their turn to be sent off to...to their destiny."

"So you are saying that this is like a revolving door. People waiting until a replacement arrives."

"Yes, that is my reasoning. Much better word," Manuel smiled and looked out into *Here*, "When I arrived, there were fields of wheat as far as the eye could see beyond the city. Now they are gone and so has much of the city." Tony looked out again and thought for a moment. Just as he took in a breath to ask another question, Manuel continued. "The ones that have stayed died by dreams of fire it seems. Violent deaths. They have not moved on."

Tony immediately snapped his gaze back to Manuel, "Dreams of fire?"

"Si, all I have spoken with, and who do not seem to be moving on, have all been brought here after horrific nightmares of fire, just like myself."

Tony was discovering that Manuel was a fountain of information.

Tony grabbed Manuel's arm and led him inside to the grand ballroom and found a small table flanked by Louis XVI chairs. Sitting down, Tony took time to explain the events of his previous life with Peter and Nancy, and explained about Fritz and his experiments. Manuel sat facing Tony and took in the tale.

Tony leaned back amazed and impressed that Manuel had not interrupted him during his soliloquy.

"I was one of this Fritz's experiments while in Costa Rica," Manuel began. "Your words have made this much clearer. This Fritz has been making moves like a chess game.

Recently, he has moved his queen into a check position threatening the king and us in here. Although I don't think he knows the extent of the damage he is inflicting, or that *Here* exists."

Tony shifted his weight in his chair. Manuel leaned in close to Tony, "I think it would be prudent to talk to your friend Peter about what is happening here."

Tony's eyes opened wider with thoughts quickly going through his mind. Was the man a madman, insane, delusional?

"Contact?" he said slowly, "I could talk to Peter? How?"

"Why of course, I have been talking to my friend Luis in his dreams several times now."

"Well of course you would have," Tony replied slowly shaking his head in amazement.

The phone sat on a small antique table. Seated in a frayed old armchair, Luis stared at it, willing it to ring. The time was near and he was very anxious but also experienced a sense of remorse. Remorse, as he knew that Manuel was most probably dead. He had had the strangest dreams over the last few nights. Dreams of Manuel talking to him, guiding him to where he was. The dreams were disjointed. Manuel drifted in and out almost trying to have Luis follow him through the dream. He had tried so hard to follow, but it seemed that the more he tried, the more distant Manuel became. Finally, last night, he had decided to just relax and let the dream unfold .

He followed Manuel through a labyrinth of jumbled

snippets of different dreams. The message Manuel was trying to get across to Luis slowly became apparent. Manuel had been assaulted and kidnapped. Where was still not clear. He found himself beside a jungle-lined road in complete darkness. Manuel was nowhere in sight, and the nocturnal sounds put him on edge. He couldn't see more than twenty feet ahead of himself. He just stood there for a few minutes with a growing sense of unease. Then, Luis almost jumped out of his skin as a jet helicopter came over the treetops behind him and quickly crossed the roadway to vanish over the next tree line.

In that brief moment, though, the lights of the helicopter had lit up his surroundings like daylight. Thirty feet down the road he saw, in a flash, a large rock. The rock made him snicker as it looked like the giant head of a baboon. He then woke up, startled, like when hearing a noise in a deep sleep. The next morning he called Ernesto, his cousin, and explained the dream. Ernesto was a bit skeptical but put out a radio message to his men to look out for that rock.

A few hours later, one of his patrols had sighted the rock and radioed back his position. Ernesto drove out to the location to check it out himself. He stopped behind the other patrol car on the side of a desolate and seldom used road near the coast. Choked with jungle, you couldn't see even a few feet in.

"There is a narrow vehicle path back about sixty feet that looks like it has had recent heavy vehicle traffic. It is on the west side heading toward the coast," stated the young trooper excitedly in a thick Spanish accent.

"Well then, Juan, let's just have a look-see," Ernesto said. They decided to go on foot since the road into the jungle was so narrow. Better to be quiet and quick to hide other than maybe driving into something nasty.

They walked down the main road to the jungle entrance and peered down. The road went straight in for about fifty feet before turning right, it looked like. They both looked at each other and then checked to see if the safeties were off on their pump-action shotguns. They walked side by side down the narrow road. The sounds of the jungle were now more intense as it closed in. Ernesto glanced at Juan, noticing that his original excitement was quickly changing into a tense awareness of his surroundings. They walked up to the curve cautiously and looked to the right. The road went another fifty feet and then turned left toward the coast. They continued on even more cautiously as they could not see the main road any longer.

Halfway down the second leg, Ernesto got a really bad feeling about all of this. The jungle had become quieter suddenly and he increased the grip on his shotgun and instinctively began to crouch, as he kept moving forward. The trooper beside him felt Ernesto's uneasiness and mirrored his boss. They came to the next turn and noticed that it went a complete 180 degrees back in the opposite direction. Ernesto knew that though the jungle was thick here, there was no physical reason that the road had to follow this path. It should go straight through to the coast. He whispered to his trooper that this was not good and to stop. They crouched there for a few seconds listening for anything. The only sound was of a vehicle slowing down

ERIK GRAHAM

on the main road, probably checking out their two patrol cars.

"Let's go back," he said quietly, slowly turning around. Unbeknownst to them, their approach had triggered two laser detection systems, one at the curve of the first bend and then half way up the second leg. As soon as the first one had been triggered, it had alerted the agents in the compound. The second trigger was confirmation of an intruder of some sort. Two CSU teams of two men each had been dispatched quietly through cut paths in the jungle. Team A, now at the edge of the jungle at the first curve, basically cut off any escape. The second team was at the edge of the jungle at the 180-degree turn. They were surrounded. Even though they did not know it yet, Ernesto sensed it.

"You watch our back," Ernesto said to his trooper beside him as they slowly backed down the road.

The view from Team A was almost like watching a picture on a shaky hand cam. They were still in the side-brush looking out between the leaves trying to get a good view. They saw two uniformed policemen with shotguns, moving their heads around nervously. The one who was overweight faced them, tense as hell. The other had his back to them. Team B, still in the brush, also saw a similar version only the person facing them was a young policeman holding his shotgun with shaking hands. This would be either a quick takedown or a messy in-close fight. The Team B leader did not like closed-in fighting with shotguns - too many variables. A member of each team now had a bead on one of the policemen. Quiet information was shared back

170

and forth with the decision to take them down when they hit the middle of the second leg of the path.

"Ten feet," was spoken by Team A's leader with only a double click received as a confirmation.

Sweat was beading all over Ernesto's forehead. He was scared shitless. He had only felt like this once before in his life, pinned down in a firefight in Panama during the US takedown of Noriega.

"Three feet," said the Team A leader and another double click was the response. The agent to his right tensed as he sighted on the overweight policeman's chest and brought his finger to the trigger waiting for the go ahead. The team leader took a final glance and...

"Ernesto!" A loud yell came from the main road.

"Hold! Hold position!" Immediately came from the Team Leader still in a quiet tone. A double click responded.

Ernesto froze and then straightened up. "Hector!" he yelled in reply. A wave of relief washed over him, "Hector, stay there. We will be right out!" Both men, still vigilant, picked up their pace and rounded the turn to see Hector, a fellow policeman who had pulled up behind the other two cars up at the main road. As Ernesto got closer, Hector could smell the fear on both of them.

"Is everything all right?" Hector asked.

"Yes, fine. Let's go," Ernesto said quietly while he herded the other two to the squad cars. A wave of unexpected nausea hit him as he approached his car. His knees almost buckled as he tried to fumble the keys into the door lock. Finally, sitting inside, he grabbed the steering wheel with both hands and rested his sweaty forehead on top of the wheel and took in a deep breath, his eyes closed. As he heard the other two cars start up he lifted his head, looked straight ahead and moved his right hand to the key and fired up the ignition. He placed the car in gear and started driving away, filled with a keen awareness of how close he had come to death. He grabbed his car phone and hit a speed dial number.

"Carlos? Carlos do you hear me?" Crappy communications here he thought, "Yes, it is me. Listen to me now. I want you to get the SIG unit ready for a night assault."

He paused as Carlos replied.

"Don't worry about that now. Just get them ready at the station. Ok?" Ernesto hung up after Carlos acknowledged. His next call was placed to Luis. He explained what had happened and that he was sending in his SIG unit that night. He told Luis to stay by the phone tonight.

As Luis sat beside the phone and kept his vigil waiting for the call, he noticed that the night sky was now darker than he could ever remember.

CHAPTER TWENTY-SEVEN

"Jesus Christ Ted, this guy is out of control!" Jack screamed to ensure he was heard. He was in Beijing traffic and his cell phone crackled a few times as he passed through different cell sites. Jack could only hear some of the words.

"Zurich is in....thirty thousand dead....," came from the receiver.

"I know that, you dumb ass. Over one hundred thousand worldwide. There is even talk that an energy weapon was being used on Zurich. An energy weapon for Christ sake. We have to contain this now, Ted. Shut it down and clean it up. Do what you need to do and use whatever means at your disposal."

Sure, Ted thought, Oh pretty please clean up the mess and I'm the dumb ass in the boss's eyes. Ted rested his chin in his palm as Jack kept spewing orders over the phone. In the background a national news service, CNE News, was showing a full news report from last night's events. Zurich was almost leveled by an inferno, the likes of which had never been seen before. The markets had taken a huge beating when they opened. The Swiss Franc had plummeted on the Forex market. Worldwide recession was being talked about especially since it was not contained to Zurich. It was as if a small percentage of the globe was on fire. They really had opened a Pandora's box this time.

"I want him gone, never to exist. Ted, do you hear me?" Jack continued on as Ted agreed.

"Yes Jack, I'll take care of it."

"You fucking better take…," silence enveloped Ted's office. Ah, thank technology again, Ted thought, for bad cell connections.

Nighttime in Costa Rica is very peaceful beside the Pacific Ocean, the teak and palm trees gently dancing in the wind. The only sounds are of surf and the rustling of leaves. The creatures sleep, except for those aware. And Fritz was very aware even at three in the morning. Although old in most respects, he was beyond most in his age bracket for assimilating technology. He had hired a young Tico computer hacker in a nearby village to hack and program some Trojan's into the communication and information databases of the Zicon compound computers. It had cost him the equivalent of a night at the movies in North America. And so, he had seen the orders come in to the compound agent's headquarters.

URGENT-URGENT-URGENT
9:00 ZULU
From: Command

To: Southern Group
    Execute Immediately – Cease all operations.
    Non-security personal to be neutralized.
    Compound to be razed to the ground.
    Scorched earth protocol.
    End Transmission.

Fritz smiled as he read the transmission supposed to be privy to only the lead agent. He had purposely had the boy hack in a command program that all communication came through him first and he could moderate them. Basically he could delete, rewrite or pass them on. He delayed this communication for now. His next order of business was to eliminate all the agents stationed at the compound.

He had worked it out, but it was going to be a matter of timing. Looking at his control panel, he paused to stare at the switch that would set everything in motion. He got up and poured himself a double dram of his favorite single malt in a very old and well-used crystal tumbler. He went back to the panel, scotch in hand and was reaching for the switch when suddenly he heard the sound of a short burst from a fully automatic rifle in the near distance. Within a micro-second; a longer burst from a larger caliber automatic, that he knew came from one of the agents, went off closer than the first.

Fritz mentally changed gears. Quickly putting down the scotch, he moved to the light switch and turned it off, giving the room an eerie effect from the illuminated control panel. By then the regular staccato of automatic fire and shouting filled the air. Fritz decided to sit in his lounge chair and wait it out. Sitting in the dark, thirty seconds later he heard the fast and heavy footfalls of the two agents that patrolled the beach area, heading toward the jungle road entrance.

Ernesto sat in the control van, which also served double duty as the area's paddy wagon rounding up drunks. His tactical force was part of the Costa Rican Special Intervention Guard (SIG). It was made up of eight young and eager police officers. Being the only experienced soldier in this section of the police force, Ernesto had set up a rigorous training program over the last few months for just such an operation. Since Costa Rica abolished its army back in 1949, the police force and SIG were the only firepower in the region and he wasn't willing to have untrained tactical officers in this area. Way too many bad hombres, was his saying over the years.

Ernesto had set up his SIG in two units of four officers each; responding to the designation of SIG 1 and SIG 2 when out in the field. He had outfitted his men with flak jackets, dark clothing and helmets wired with two-way communication. Ernesto had also stretched his budget to outfit all eight with night vision goggles, which had already proved useful in the last four deployments.

Ernesto sent them in at three in the morning, figuring that was the best moment. Most would be asleep at that time. The teams stepped into the jungle on opposite sides of the road entrance, about a 150 feet apart. They each went in a cross formation. One leading, two behind a few paces to the right and left of him, with the fourth trailing behind.

This was their territory. They knew the terrain even though they had not been in this part of the jungle before. SIG 1 was to the left of the entrance, moving forward quietly as possible. SIG 2 had gone in to the right of the entrance and stopped at the 50 foot mark, at the exact point where Ernesto and his younger partner Juan, the leader of SIG 2, had had to back down earlier.

Through the night vision glasses, Juan now saw the infrared beam across the road that they had tripped. Ernesto had been right about it. Amateur, he thought of himself.

Juan leader radioed Ernesto about their find and reported that they would skirt around the road to the right, following the jungle.

SIG 1 was now 100 feet in when they first encountered trouble. In the blink of an eye, both SIG 1 and SIG 2's communications went out. They both stopped immediately and regrouped around each unit's leader.

Ernesto was frantic as he tried to re-establish communication. Both units now, even more cautious, continued on in a single line formation with one man at point.

SIG 2's point man slowly crept along still in the jungle as they rounded the 180 degree curve on the road and headed back toward the coast. The jungle was not as thick at this point and the view from his night vision goggles was surreal. He stopped and raised a fist motioning his followers

ERIK GRAHAM

to stop also. He scanned the area, the goggles giving his eyesight a green landscape. The road was empty and the jungle was gently swaying in the night breeze. And then he saw it, the outline of a helmet behind a bunch of large ferns. The next few seconds slowed down as he raised his rifle to sight the helmet. He saw his adversary doing the same. He had a half second advantage and squeezed the trigger for a short burst. All he saw was the snap of a head.

The spray of blood hit his cheek as the bullet impacted the CSU agent's head right beside him. The agent toppled to the jungle floor. Immediately, another agent raised his rifle and fired a long burst in front of him. The jungle was awakened; monkey's screeching and scurrying around.

The sound of bullets whizzed by Ernesto's SIG 2 Unit as the echo of the reports bounced back from the tops of the trees. A loud smack behind the unit's point man made him turn to see his tail man sprawled on the jungle floor, bleeding from a head wound. The firefight stopped as they lost sight of each other. Both opposing forces silently advanced on each other. As if aware of the danger within, the jungle had gone silent as well.

The CSU agents of Team B had circled more to the left to cut down the ambient light bouncing off the road. Only three large teak trees now separated the two groups.

As SIG 2's three remaining officers reached the trees, the three surviving CSU agents came out from around them. What followed was an all-out slugfest of subsonic projectiles. They all saw each other at the same time due

178

to the limited vision of the goggles. Fingers rammed the triggers simultaneously and each started spraying bullets in an arc. The noise was deafening, even drowning out the grunts and screams as the slugs found their targets. Within seconds all was quiet, only the haze of gun smoke hovered over the mangled dead bodies.

CSU Team A's leader anxiously tried to establish contact with Team B. All he got was static. He immediately contacted the two agents stationed near the beach.

"Any contact with hostiles?" he asked, as quietly as he could.

"None," replied the agent at the beach.

"Team B is not responding, move up toward Team B's last position double time."

Two minutes later Fritz heard the hurried boots run by from the beach.

With both SIG 2 and the CSU Team B eliminated, CSU Team A and the only remaining SIG 1 Unit were now at a stand-still, only 200 feet apart, hidden from each other. The sound of gunfire and screams to the north had frozen both of them. The two beach agents, now designated as CSU Team C, moved in defensively. They entered the jungle from the compound clearing just west of Team B's last reported position, led by the still activated GPS tracking device still attached to dead Team B leader's belt. It took another three minutes to reach the signal's position. Already a swarm of flies had descended on the bodies.

"Team B has been eliminated," Team C's senior agent reported and continued, "Looks like four police assault troops are also dead. They must have run into each other," he said shakingly.

"OK, get a GPS fix on me and circle around up near the main road and come at a southwest angle toward us. I think there is another group of police officers in the middle between my position and the main road," stated Team A's leader.

"Copy," was the reply.

The next four minutes were tense for all three groups. The leader of the remaining Police SIG 1 unit was really scared. No communications, no knowledge if the other unit was still advancing. His biggest fear was that he could feel he was being trapped. That feeling gave him the determination to move on. Determination that, if this was to be his last night on this planet, well then, he was going to bring some along with him.

He signaled for two of the SIG 1 officers to follow him forward. He then sent the fourth officer 60 feet up the left side, to circle and maybe flank the enemy he could sense in front of them. He determined that he needed as much firepower as possible up front, so he deployed the two remaining officers on either side of him up about 10 feet. They proceeded slowly, creeping along, stopping and listening.

The sudden squeal of a monkey behind him to the right startled the SIG 1 Unit Leader and froze him to the spot. He sensed a trap and quickly adjusted his game plan accordingly. He told the two men beside him to keep moving forward while he would retreat and then circle to the right, the same way he had sent his fourth man. Unconventional, splitting up his men in this way, but hearing no sounds from the other unit drove him to protect his flank.

The jungle was deathly silent again, but that did not mean it was static. Thousands, maybe millions of creatures moved around in their own nocturnal dance. One near the top of the food chain slithered along the jungle floor. The cobra was immense as it moved along in its hypnotic S-pattern. Its path became a dividing line. A line separating opposing forces. The lone SIG 1 Unit Leader checked his flank but didn't even see the snake 100 feet to his left, and neither did Team C's two agents, heading in the opposite direction of the still moving snake. So, like the old expression of two ships passing in the night, they continued on oblivious of each other.

The lone SIG 1 officer, sent to flank the enemy in front, had crept up as silently as he could. Now situated behind and to the left of CSU Team A, he could see a head or two of his opposing force hidden behind thick foliage. He needed to get closer. He took a moment to wipe the sweat build-up on his forehead and dripping into his eyes. The jungle humidity was stifling, even at this time of the morning. He got down on his knees and proceeded to crawl forward, trying his best not to move the large leaves that seemed to be everywhere. He still could not see his enemy but took a bead on a large teak tree standing thirty feet directly behind them.

The two SIG 1 officers ordered to go forward had crept along, more scared to death with each step they took.

"Movement detected at about 50 feet east of our position," stated the Team A's leader through his COM unit.

Team C's response was, "Confirmed. We see two targets heading straight for you. They are 60 feet south from our position. We will close in." A double click was the response.

By now the lone SIG 1 officer had crawled up to the tree and caught his breath, trying to calm himself.

The SIG 1 Unit Leader, nearing the road, was getting worried as he had not made contact with any opposition and had gone too far back. They had passed him somehow. He turned and headed back.

The four agents of CSU Team A had their rifles at the ready position, scanning the area with their scopes. They had seen movement for a brief second. The two SIG 1 officers had also seen them and had dropped to the jungle floor. They crawled forward, slowly closing the gap.

The CSU agent located on the far left of the team tensely

scanned the forty-five degree section he was responsible for. They had stayed in this one place too long, he thought, but he was not the leader here. He didn't realize that the jungle also recognized that they had been stationery for too long. A black widow spider, one of the deadliest around, found his nylon webbing and flak jacket a unique surface to explore. Its long furry legs moved stealth-like up the agent's back. It stopped in a couple of places when the jacket material moved with the man.

When they first sighted the two officers in front of them, the CSU team had snapped up their rifles to eyesight. This had jarred the spider and it sunk its fangs into the flak jacket with no effect. The jacket kept moving side-to-side irritating the spider and it climbed up over the collar and onto exposed flesh at the base of the skull. The spider sensing a softer surface attacked again, sinking its small but deadly fangs deep into the hot sweaty flesh.

The result was spectacular. The team agent, who had a finger on the trigger, involuntarily squeezed it while letting out a blood-curdling scream. He released his left hand from the rifle stock and reached back to protect his injured area. His rifle on full automatic erupted in sound and tracer bullets that arced to the right almost cutting down his own men. Instinctively, the other three started firing blindly into the jungle.

The two SIG 1 officers, already on the ground, heard and felt round after round go over their heads. One of them flipped on his back, took out a hand grenade, pulled the pin and threw it over his head toward the gunfire.

The lone SIG 1 officer had been positioned behind the CSU agents and was now out from behind the tree with his gun raised. He started firing at his enemy from left to right just as the grenade exploded above all of them.

As soon as the grenade went off, both SIG 1 officers raised their rifles and sprayed the forward area with automatic fire. The jungle became a bizarre light show of muzzle flashes and tracer bullets piercing through smoke.

It took little time for Team C, coming from the north, to home in on the SIG 1 officers' muzzle flashes. They then started their own light show, shredding the area ahead of them with volley after volley. Within seconds, all was quiet again.

"Report in," came a strangled request from CSU Team A's leader.

"Team C here," was the only reply.

The Team A's leader swung around and saw his three team agents sprawled on the ground with various wounds from the shrapnel of the grenade. He saw no movement, only death. As he scanned the area, he came upon the lone SIG 1 officer, also lying lifeless on his back. Two bullet entries in his head and neck, with some shrapnel mixed in. Must have been hit by his own guys, he surmised as a wave of pain washed up his left leg. Obviously, he had taken a large piece of that grenade as well. Team C joined him by then and reported that the two SIG 1 officers in front of them were also dead.

"Ok, let's get back to the command center now! We need to call in back-up right now and I need an evac to a hospital," the leader yelled as they helped him up.

In the meantime, the SIG 1 Unit Leader, still on his own and trying to find his unit, was by now questioning the wisdom of his decision to separate his group as he had heard the fight where he had left his men. As he finally came across his two dead officers, he allowed himself a moment of deep guilt and sorrow. He retreated back slowly for ten feet and checked the area visually. then double-timed it back toward the road. He broke out of the jungle near the van to be confronted with a shotgun. Ernesto sighed in relief and lowered his weapon. The SIG 1 Unit Leader didn't hesitate as he jumped into the van yelling, "Let's get the fuck out of here."

The remaining three CSU Agents rounded the command center's building and half ran with their leader between them to the door and then inside. Fritz, now back to the window, smiled to himself as he saw the agents enter the command center.

"Just a moment longer," he said to himself as took the last swig of his scotch and finally flicked the switch. He couldn't hear its effectiveness as it was too far away, but he did see one of the men in the control room clawing at the window in vain. The cylinder of cyanide he had placed there a month ago took quick action on the last of the Zicon CSU agents station there.

"Now to finish the Führer's work," Fritz said as headed to the main terminal and started entering data.

CHAPTER TWENTY-EIGHT

Six miles up over the Atlantic, the sleek airliner streamed along toward Bern, Switzerland. Nancy and Peter had lucked out once more and had been upgraded to first class at the last minute. Economy had been fully booked. Nancy had shamelessly flirted with the clerk when they bought the tickets in Montreal. "Quebecois men are so predictable," she had said to Peter. Nancy had also surprised Peter by using a special credit card that was tied to an offshore trust. She told him it had been set up by a now dead but extremely rich relative. There was no name on the card and all purchases were routed through two banks, making detection extremely difficult. Good thing, Peter had thought at the time, that they both had kept their valuables in the lab's safe. Nancy had surprised him again; here was a very wealthy girl who did not want the trappings of wealth. She wanted to work with him. She admitted that this was only the second time she had used the card, almost forgetting about the untold bank balance that she had at her disposal.

Peter was pressed up against the windowpane with a

pillow propped in between. Nancy's head rested in his lap as she curled up into a small ball and slept. Peter's left hand twitched as he sank into his dreams, utterly exhausted from the events of the past 48 hours.

Landing in his dream, Peter saw a myriad of faded, obscure colors, like an old-school LSD trip he had once tried in university. He started walking down a deserted city street which had just appeared in his vision. Looking up, he saw dozens and dozens of various discarded shoes, sneakers and boots hung by their tied laces. They were strung over the wires between poles on a never-ending road.

There was not a sound, not even of his footsteps as he walked down the center of the yellow-lined road. Rounding a corner, Peter stopped short. The road continued on into the horizon but then suspended into nothingness. No more buildings, and the poles no longer existed, just the unending road. A sense of panic came over him. Turning around to go back, he found himself blocked by a sheer rock face. Peter looked up the cliff and could not see the top of it. The way back had now vanished.

Trapped in his own dream, Peter walked on for a minute or so. He then sat down cross-legged on the asphalt totally frustrated. Trying to wake himself up was not working.

Like he could ever do it in the past, he thought.

Deciding to just wait this out, he just sat there. Moments later, he heard a rumbling noise behind him and as he looked over his shoulder he saw that the cliff was now moving toward him.

"Ok, ok, I'll get off my ass," Peter said out loud and got up and started walking again. The road was still there, but up ahead he could see that the ground beside the road just fell away. Walking along, still on the road, he reached the end of the ground. As he stood at the edge of the ground he looked up and saw blue sky with no clouds, and then looking below where the ground ended, he saw the same. The road still went out into the nothingness of the sky. It just never ended. He stepped gingerly onto the part of the road that was suspended in air, at first believing that it would collapse. After the first five steps, Peter relaxed and instinctively looked back again. The road stretched back into blue sky, the cliff gone. He was on a ribbon of asphalt. Deciding to just keep walking forward, he actually started enjoying himself. After walking and walking, a hill appeared on the horizon. A tubular structure looking like a very modern dwelling stood over the crest. Even though it was still very far away, Peter was relieved and wondered where this dream would end up.

From the base of the hill a gold shimmering form approached. Peter slowed down his pace, squinting to discern the apparition. Peter looked in awe as the form moved down the road coming toward him. Shaped like a lion, no fur to be seen...only a golden flame. Flame? Peter stopped quickly assessing it as a threat. Sure looks like one, he answered himself. The lion torch kept advancing at a steady pace dead center to where Peter was situated. That is when he started feeling its heat.

Now Peter really started panicking. Fritz was here. He could sense his presence implicitly. For the first time on the road, Peter turned and started to go back. The lion torch did not register the change as it continued its advance, never taking its blood red eyes off Peter. Showing more bravado than he thought possible, Peter increased his pace. The tension in his mind for the next few moments was excruciating.

Was it still there? Was it closer? he thought.

Weighing the decision to look back or not, Peter lost the battle and took a quick glance. The lion torch was at the same distance as before and keeping Peter's pace. Peter walked for what felt like an hour, stealing glances backward, the torch still in pursuit, the dwelling shrinking back into the horizon.

Why can't I wake up? he thought. Mindlessly walking down the road, his heart jumped as two identical lion torches floated towards the road in front of him. His escape from either side was now gone. Now stopping, Peter felt heat again on his front and back as the torches bore down on him.

"Fucked," was his retort to himself.

Like a baseball player caught between two bases, Peter looked back and forth as the heat continued to rise around him.

"No, no, no…not here. Not like this. Owww!" Peter said as his hand brushed one of the heated rivets in his jeans.

"Ok, this is not funny anymore!" he said. His mind working quickly, he analyzed his options. They were few but the heat was not unbearable yet. Trying to use surprise as an advantage, Peter turned and ran towards one of the torches. Immediately, like they were somehow connected by his actions, they both started sprinting towards him. Peter ran with all his might hoping to run through the apparition. With only three feet between them, Peter's arm hair started curling in the heat. Instinctively, Peter tried to cover his bare arms. Twisting in pain he fell to his knees, now aware of what Tony's ordeal may have felt like. As he fell, one of his knees collapsed and sent him into a roll. A roll that sent Peter sailing off the road. Off the road, now pain free, he free-fell into the nothingness of blue sky.

CHAPTER TWENTY-NINE

Peter heard a voice.

"Peter, Peter, wake up...wake up now!" it screamed.

Wow, just like deja-vue, he thought, Nancy in the lab.

"Peter Sutherland. Wake up now!" she said.

Peter's body was pushed against the glass as he was prodded. Slowly Peter opened his eyes. Thank God, he thought. I am back on the plane.

Peter looked down only to see Nancy still asleep in his lap.

"Hello, old friend," came a familiar voice.

"I am still dreaming right...Tony?" Peter said slowly now looking at the flight attendant. Tony was probably the largest flight attendant the industry would ever allow if this were reality.

"Yes, my man. You are still dreaming, but now you have a guide."

"Excellent. I surely did not have one the last episode I just went through."

"Yes, Fritz is up to his old tricks again. Good thing I twisted that roadway to one side."

"You did that?"

"Why not? It was part of my dream."

"Your dream?" Peter was still sitting down with Nancy on his lap.

"Follow me my friend," Tony quipped as he held out his hand to help Peter out of his seat. Moving into the aisle Peter noticed that all the passengers were sleeping and that blackness surrounded the cabin. Peter followed Tony down the aisle, stopping by a food cart and grabbing a muffin. Tony looked back and chuckled.

"My sudo-stomach is growling," Peter said as he raised the muffin to his mouth. He stopped in shock as he noticed the burnt hair on his arm.

"Oh shit," said Peter.

"Oh yeah," Tony said, stopping to wait, "more real than unreal is the saying, I believe."

Peter tossed the muffin away losing his appetite and continued following. Tony stopped at a space between some seats and proceeded to open the emergency door.

Peter was just about to scream a warning when stunning rays of sunshine blinded him. Tony walked out of the plane and Peter followed ending up back on the road again still suspended in mid air. This time the sky looked real, with small clouds surrounding them.

"Ok. I'm impressed. Will you please tell me what the hell is going on here?" Peter stopped.

Tony stopped and clapped twice, hard.

"What, trying to turn off the lights?" Peter yelled out behind Tony, thinking that the lights were about to go out.

Actually what happened was that the hill off near the far horizon shot toward both of them at an incredible speed and then screamed to a stop at their feet. The base of the hill was within a few steps where a well-worn stairway started. It ended at the crest a hundred feet up and came up to the tube-work of the dwelling.

"Always wanted to do that! I just changed the rules a bit" Tony said smartly and began taking the stairs two at a time.

Peter was just about to say something but had to keep pace with Tony. Coming up to the top, Peter tried to take it all in. It wasn't a dwelling after all. Peter put his hands on his hips and leaned back to take in the full view of what he called the tubes at that point. Tony walked up beside him, faced the same way and said, "This is what I have figured out so far."

After a few seconds of waiting Peter said, "Ok, I'll play along, especially since this is my dream. What have you figured out?" Peter still looked toward the tubes as Tony raised his hands and spread them apart

"Peter Sutherland this is the dreamweave," Tony turned towards Peter, looking smug.

Peter sensed that Tony was trying to show him something and followed his gaze. Tony jogged ahead and started explaining.

"All this is the dreamweave as I have seen it. See this? This is the dreamhub that I am trapped in right now."

"Trapped?" Peter questioned.

"Yes, hundreds of thousands are there including

myself. These tubes here," Tony pointed toward a series of thin tubes, "are dreamlines that I have traveled to other parts of the dreamweave."

"Hold on Tony," Peter said shaking his head. "Is this real or another dream within a dream? And if real, how are we talking right now?"

"Oh buddy, this is real. As real as real can get. Ok, the short version. Have a seat."

"But when," Peter did not get to finish. He was distracted as a comfortable leather chair appeared on the grass near him. Peter shrugged his shoulders and sat down.

Tony sitting in his own chair leaned forward and put his hands on his knees.

"I died at the hands of Fritz, you know that. What happened after is extraordinary."

Tony began explaining the glider ride to the center of the earth which turned into meeting the beautiful Being. He continued on with what he learned about *Here* from Manuel and what Fritz's experiments were doing to *Here* and about the latest energy waves.

"This is when Manuel told me how to contact you and others through dreams."

Peter jumped in, "Ok. So you died after going through Fritz's hell, ending up in a place you call *Here* and then you just happened to appear in my dream, saving my ass from Fritz?"

Tony nodded in agreement, "That's about it. Looks like the unlucky ones who die by Fritz's artificial nightmares are stuck in *Here*, well maybe not. I will explain that in a bit."

Tony shifted and crossed his legs while leaning back, "Manuel explained that though we are trapped in *Here*, we can still venture out into the dreamweave, but we always end up back *Here*. Kind of like a boomerang over an extended period. So I started jumping out from *Here* and intersecting dreamlines hoping to find you."

"That must have been easy," Peter said sarcastically.

Tony continued, "Finally I started to map this all out here, not *Here* but ....you know. Still confusing...anyway, I clued in quickly that many dreamlines were being drawn to this one point."

Tony pointed above his head to a very large hub of tubes. Thousands of other tubes seemed to be connected to it, making it looked like a spoked wheel.

"This is Fritz's negative dreamhub which has not collapsed since I've been here. I have concluded that at some point you, in your dream, would be drawn toward his neg-hub," Tony smiled using a new word in his vocabulary. "Anyway, I started intercepting dreamlines. Really just popping in to see if you were there. It seems I was just in time. I came upon lots of others that had met their demise before I came across yours."

"Ok, but how did you change my dream with yours, and for that matter how can you dream if you are dead?"

"Well it seems that Fritz, whether he knows it or not, has really screwed up the norm around here. His neg-hub and the positive hub we made back at the lab ourselves are all artificial. So it seems that with one of the artificial dead dreamers," Tony started laughing, "Sorry. This sounds too bizarre to be true, but when one of us ventures out into the dreamweave, we are forming an artificial dreamline. A dreamline that I can create myself even when I'm not dreaming. You follow?" Tony said placing his arms on the comfortable chair's armrest.

Scientist Peter now came online, "Lets back up a bit. You must have detected me in my...hmm, sub-dream. The dream I was having before this dream, walking in the city and coming across your road."

"Actually I was intercepting countless dreamlines at the time. That is why it took so long to find you. I literally found you as you were going to be lion food. The only thing I could think of was to change the road. The part you talk about walking through the city was not mine. Mine melded into yours. When you woke up in the plane, that was your dream. I just jumped in and steered you back to mine, and now to this place."

"If the road was yours, where did the lions come from?"

"From Fritz, I presume. You were, or your dreamline was, spiraling around his neg-hub being drawn in. Peter, I have to get to the point of why I contacted you. You'll soon awake."

Peter pursed his lips and nodded.

"Fritz's neg-hub has its own energy now and it is not collapsing like normal ones do. It is drawing in dreamlines from everywhere. The dream dead are all winding up in *Here,* but that is getting smaller and smaller, collapsing upon itself. We cannot last long there. Peter, our souls are on the line if this doesn't get fixed soon."

"Fixed? What in the hell can I do to fix this?" Peter said waving his arms about.

"Actually, that is what we need you to do, Peter," Tony said leaning forward and staring him straight in the eye. "We need you to bring something back to your reality, but you have to go through hell to get there." Tony smiled.

Peter felt this throat dry up instantly and gulped.

CHAPTER THIRTY

"Well it's about time, sleepy head," Nancy said in a friendly voice. Peter did a great big stretch and yawn. A pretty flight attendant walked by and reminded Peter to put up his seat as they were about to land.

"Looks like I slept across the entire Atlantic," he said casually looking out at the city of Bern, Switzerland below.

"And dinner." She turned serious, "Peter, the news reports about Zurich are frightening, but it has spread to many other parts."

Peter just looked ahead and calmly said, "It's going to get much worse unless we stop it." He yawned again. He turned his head toward her and placed his hand on hers. "Tony is trapped in the dreamweave and Fritz's neg-hub is growing stronger by the hour."

Nancy's face was blank for a moment. "You've been there, haven't you?"

Peter simply nodded and went on to describe what he had just experienced as the plane landed. A tear of joy ran down Nancy's cheek as the plane taxied in to the arrival gate. She had two reasons to rejoice now. One that Tony was still, well not still alive, but still Tony. The other thought was that although there was no proof, Peter had brought back incredible hope. Hope that all was not lost after we died; somehow we shall carry on, on to another level and or dimension.

Walking through the terminal she was still thinking of the implications of this new knowledge, oblivious to her surroundings. She finally turned to ask Peter a question when she noticed him with a crowd of onlookers back twenty feet down the corridor watching a television hanging from the ceiling.

"Peter?" she said strolling up to his side.

Peter didn't answer and just kept staring at the screen. A CNE News special report was in progress, only the way CNE News could do it during a major event. War or disaster, they always had full coverage with audio, video and dramatic commentary.

Zurich was in flames - out of control. Dozens of city blocks of residential streets were alight with fire spreading towards the banking district. Exhausted fire crews were shown overwhelmed by the intensity of the firestorm. To add to the difficulties, the reporter announced that the weather was not cooperating with any rain in sight. The report broke to images of home video shots of dozens of similar small to large fires spreading sporadically throughout the world. The so-called TV experts who were being interviewed, for once in their careers, were stymied by the events. They posed many more questions than gave answers. Conspiracy theory advocates were salivating on the different scenarios posted on Internet forums and chat rooms. The level of paranoia planet wide had risen. It could be sensed everywhere.

It surpassed the anxiety felt with the Cuban missile crisis in the 60's. Images, sounds and now smells of death and destruction filled the air to millions located near the hot spots. CNE News's coverage was the tip of the iceberg. In actuality, the problems became worse. Looting and lawlessness followed very quickly as emergency and police services were stretched to the max in the affected areas. The government of Switzerland was in turmoil. The President of the Swiss Confederation had been one of Fritz's victims as were five other key Councillors.

Though only Zurich and some small parts of Boston were the main focus, about six other major countries were affected so far. The media attention made it feel like a worldwide catastrophe.

It was Peter's turn to now look towards Nancy and find her gone, only to see her a few feet away at a public Internet terminal typing away madly. She looked up quickly when he approached.

"It's Klaus! He finally answered my e-mail. He's alive and waiting for us."

Nancy filled Peter in on where Klaus was and the facilities he had available for them. Peter sat down and squeezed in next to Nancy in the chair designed for one. For a second, sexual awareness shot through him as their bodies touched.

He refocused and nudging Nancy's hands away started typing on the keyboard.

Nancy, a little upset, looked at his face and realized she had never seen such conviction and focus in him. She swung her gaze back to Peter's efficiency on the computer and watched the monitor as he typed.

Peter's speed increased like a man on his deathbed trying to divulge his life's secrets before passing. She then realized that Peter had to put this down somewhere where there would be a record of what he had seen or felt. As she read, a better, clearer view entered her mind of what Peter had endured and she unconsciously stroked his shoulders and back like a well accustomed lover.

Minutes flew by as the paragraphs turned from explanations to directions of what Peter needed when they arrived. In his e-mail Klaus had included a description of the facilities that Werner had and the medical innovations that were at his disposal. Was it fate, Peter thought in one part of his brain, as he still pounded out his directions, or was it the global consciousness that had led all of them to this place and time?

Quickly scanning his lengthy e-mail, he hit the send button knowing that the fate of thousands, perhaps millions went with it as it went through the secured pipelines of the Internet. It was then that he sensed her near him again.

He turned his head to her, their noses inches apart.

They said nothing, for there was nothing to say. The electricity of the two in sync together was overpowering.

They both moved in simultaneously, at first softly, probing the deliciousness of their first kiss.

Rapidly they were embraced, hungrily attacking each other's lips and tongues, holding each other in an almost breathless hug. Passers-by gave various reactions from disgust to putting their arm around their own partners. Several minutes later they broke for air or maybe for another reason. They would keep that to themselves. Again, no words were spoken, just a knowing gaze into each other's eyes.

"We've got lots to do Nance. Lets go," he said sweetly as he helped her out of the booth.

Klaus had given them instructions on how to get to where he was. They arranged a taxi to the train station. The time on the rail went by quickly as Nancy sat typing out the instructions and code for what Peter proposed when they would arrive in Visp, Switzerland. It started out as a small pit in her stomach and grew as Peter went on delving further into what he was about do to. She was afraid. Fearing for the world and for someone that she truly cared for…as she always had.

The train rolled into the Visp station. They were already at the departure door and were the first off. Klaus had told them that transportation would be provided for them. Within a minute, a large smartly dressed man approached them as they exited the station's train platform and stated authoritatively in a thick German accent, "Follow me please." He took Peter's arm non-threateningly. Nancy in tow kept up with the men weaving through the station to a waiting limousine.

A driver quickly opened the back door for the couple. In a flash they were seated, the door closing behind them. When they looked forward they were staring down the barrel of a pistol.

"Herr Sutherland, Fraulein Anderson. It is a pleasure to finally meet you. You have been very persistent," he paused. "Let me introduce myself. My name is Fritz Rhinefalt."

The color in both Peter and Nancy's faces paled immediately.

He pulled out a cigar, keeping quiet. Placing it on his lips he turned the pistol towards himself and pulled the trigger. Both jumped at the sight of flame coming from its end, lighting the big cigar.

"Actually, I'm Klaus," he started laughing, "and they say German's have no sense of humor." He laughed louder as Peter and Nancy looked at one another with huge wide eyes as the limo pulled out into traffic.

CHAPTER THIRTY-ONE

The hour was approaching. Fritz sat on the small thatch roofed porch listening to jazz magic playing on his small sound system. He had a lit Cuban cigar in his right hand, which was one of his occasional indulges. It wouldn't be long before Zicon sent more agents to find out why no communication came from the compound. His compound. He had heard the requests over the communication board, but he simply ignored proper communication codes or phrases.

His mind drifted back to one of his best-remembered days over his long life. The day the Führer had pinned the German Order to his black SS uniform and the shaking of his hand in front of Goebbels and Himmler. The Führer pronounced to all in the room that he, Fritz Rhinefalt, was going to be responsible for a destructive force that would engulf the enemies of the thousand-year Reich. His name would be known beside the great men standing with him.

Fritz took another pull of the cigar and slowly exhaled.

"Well, Mein Führer," he said to the empty courtyard,

"it took another sixty years to finish what we started, but tonight I will unleash that destruction you prophesied on that great day."

Fritz's left hand came up from the armrest of his chair and lifted up the iron cross still attached to his uniform. Moths had taken their toll, but Fritz had still brought out the jacket one last time. The SS jacket was loose on his frail frame but it still commanded respect and fear.

A buzzer went off inside and Fritz pushed himself off the chair and sauntered into the lab's control room. A muted television was mounted high in a corner of the room, showing the shocking images of uncontrollable fires in urban centers. CNE News started a special report with a foreboding title of "The Apocalypse Has Come?"

Fritz paid no mind to it as the same news bites simply rotated until more ammunition was found to feed the news junkies.

Well, he thought, let's see if this will change their tune.

The control panel was now like an old friend. How many times had he started this process? For a second, only a second, he hesitated. How much pain have I inflicted? Fritz caught himself staring at a panel monitor as an ash from his still-smoldering cigar fell to the floor.

The coordinates had already been set, waiting for the perfect time. It was so German in the planning and execution. He placed his thumb over a large red button. He chuckled, thinking back. He had demanded it be built that way for nostalgia's sake, the Big Red button as it had been in the history of movies and television for years. Putting down his cigar on the counter, not caring if it burnt to its finish, he stroked his stubbled chin for a few moments and pushed down hard on the button.

Fritz stood motionless for a minute, then reached into his tunic and brought out a fresh Cuban. Using an old cutter, he nipped one end and then lit the other end. Taking a long pull, he turned and walked out, going across the courtyard toward the worn path to the beach.

She had fallen asleep after the lengthy session in bed. Only a bed sheet covered her from the small of her back downward. The hotel room was still chilly from the constant drone of the air conditioning unit.

Jack sat propped up against the headboard having a smoke. He looked down at the girl, barely eighteen. She had been pretty good, but I was better, he thought. He was still trying to convince himself of his virility since his 'she' had moved on.

"Fuck. Dead and still haunting me," he said quietly to himself.

Getting up to go to the window, a wave of nausea overtook him. He stopped and rested against a chair until it passed. He slowly approached the window, gently holding his stomach.

Still a six-pack. Gotta keep that up, he thought as he rubbed it.

He looked out toward the city of Beijing, the night broken up by the city lights. The girl moaned behind him

"Ya baby, still dreaming about me, huh?" he said still staring out the window.

He stood there finishing his smoke, thinking about his next takeover bid meeting in the morning. I'll make them bleed, he thought randomly.

He put out his cigarette and looked out over the city once again. Smoke was coming from one section of the city and emergency vehicles could be seen rushing toward it. He spotted flame now and focused closer on it. His brain registered danger just as the hotel fire alarm began its toll.

Jack whirled around just as he realized the flame was a reflection from inside the window. The girl was alight with a small amount of smoke already rising from her body.

He stumbled sideways away from her as she started to scream. That unearthly scream he had heard before. He ran toward the door of the room, grabbing his shirt on the way, no time to find his shoes.

Dressed in only his jockeys and shirt, he opened the door only to be pushed back by the smoke in the hallway. He quickly closed the door and ran to the washroom. He soaked one of the large hotel towels in cold water, trying to ignore the sounds of agony in the next room.

Jack's mind raced with thoughts of revenge. He knew Fritz was responsible. He went back to the room door. This time he knelt with the towel wrapped around his head. Slowly he opened the door to discover that the smoke was thicker now, billowing inside. A small amount of cleaner air rested on the floor. Jack went left toward the stairway exit he had quickly scanned on the room door Fire Panel.

Groping along the long hallway, he shuddered as he passed some rooms, the same haunting sounds emitting from within. Three rooms from the exit, Jack looked back as the sound of a primal scream and footsteps came behind him. His breathing through the towel began to get harder. His vision caught the glimpse of legs from the knees down as the smoke was too thick to see above. They were old withered legs, running in a scattered pattern.

As the legs came closer, the person ran straight into a wall and got turned around, now starting to head back toward where it started. Jack, for a brief break in the smoke saw a melted form, the mouth just a hole, arms flaying. He involuntarily shuddered and crawled towards the exit.

After what seemed like an eternity, he reached the exit door and, turning the knob, fell into the stairway landing. With the door closed behind him, he saw hope as the stairway was pretty much clear of smoke. He wasted no time on his trek down from the fourteenth floor. The concrete steps cutting into his feet giving him more resolve of what he was planning for Fritz.

He had never actually killed another person himself, but he started relishing the thought as he descended floor by floor.

At the ninth floor he stopped and tried the door only to find it locked, only accessible from the hallways. He continued down, now hearing other voices and footfalls in the stairway. Running down the last few flights Jack came to the bottom exit door. Hitting the large exit bar in the middle, he slammed into the door, only to be thrown back.

The door did not budge.

Picking himself up, he hit the bar again and again with the same result. He started kicking it, blood staining the lower part of the door from his cut feet. Rage took over Jack as he relentlessly punished the door for not opening. A smaller older man came around the corner, dressed in flannel pajamas and soot around his eyes and mouth. He instinctively joined in with Jack on the assault of the door. Another victim came upon them and the three now used their shoulders in unison, but to no avail. Within minutes the bottom landing was crowded with panicked people. More and more came toward the landing as the sixty-story hotel started to burn.

Jack's focus shifted from the door to the crush of people pressing him against it. At first he simply used his strength at pushing back, but the numbers grew. He heard yelling from above as more came down to what must be the only exit. The older man that had first helped him was wide-eyed with fear and pain as he was being crushed, the bar now becoming part of him.

Savagely, Jack started to fight the people back with fists and legs. It gave him a bit of reprieve as the crowd reeled back, only to be pushed harder forward from the momentum still coming down the stairs. Jack's arms were pushed down as several bodies slammed into him. Nails dug into his face from a woman he had just hit. No distinctive voices could be made out as only the sounds of humans in a death struggle bounced from the now bloodstained concrete walls. The staircase had become a death chamber.

Jack could not comprehend was what happening. His face was ravaged by any who could get close trying to escape. Jack took the blows, his arms and legs pinned. He was unable to turn and face the door. Images of his life began flashing before his eyes, now swollen shut from the attacks. The crush was now almost unbearable. His breathing became almost non-existent.

To suffocate out of water, he thought. "Fuck you, Fritz!" he screamed with his last breath, as he collapsed wedged against the door.

CHAPTER THIRTY-TWO

The ride from the train station had been productive even after the initial shock of Klaus's humor. Driving through the outskirts of the small city, Nancy and Peter both fell into a collaborative mode when Klaus, taking a pull from his cigar now and then, updated them on the equipment and set up he had worked on with his friend Werner.

"I am still at a loss at what you think you will be able to accomplish here Peter," Klaus said concerned. "We set up one area of Werners's lab into what I'm calling the 'dreaming den'. All the comforts of home and life saving equipment are at your disposal," he went on sarcastically, "even if I have to bring you back from the dead."

"Yes actually," Peter retorted, as Nancy just gulped, "there is a good chance. I'd say eighty percent chance that it will be needed. According to Tony, Fritz's neg-hub is not dissipating and is actually growing. Since he has been going after us individually, he has put the whole world in peril." He paused and stroked his stubbly chin, "Fritz, whether he knows it or not, has also put a place called *Here* in jeopardy."

"Here? Where is that?" Klaus asked suspiciously.

Peter then updated Klaus on what he had not covered in the e-mail. Klaus crossed one of his legs and took another drag on his cigar, letting this all soak in.

"A gateway to the afterlife?" Klaus murmured.

"Isn't it wonderful?" Nancy chipped in.

"So Peter, Master of Dreams, how do we go about saving everyone and *Here*?"

Peter explained his plan as the limo turned down a private gravel road.

The car traveled through old growth trees for a mile until it broke out into an opening. Nancy stifled a gasp.

"It is wonderful, yes?" Klaus said more as a statement.

The two guests simply stared at the grand mansion on top of a small hill.

"More like a fairytale," Nancy replied. The limo came up the hill and rounded a large circular driveway.

"Werner has his lab set up in the back part of the estate. His ancestors had good genes."

"I'll say," Peter almost whistled.

The limo did not stop at the front but proceeded down a small paved road and within minutes, they saw a two-story high-tech looking building surrounded by forest. As the limo pulled up to the front, a tall wiry older man was pacing outside.

As they got out of the limo, Klaus was about to

introduce their host, but before he could do so, Werner started talking excitedly.

"He is at it again, Klaus," Werner exclaimed while wheeling himself around and heading towards the buildings front door. "Beijing is in flames and more hot spots around the planet are popping up."

Klaus stopped, smiled and turned to Peter and Nancy, "My friend Werner," he said extending his arm to open the door as a valet.

"Beijing?" Peter questioned, following Werner who was now fidgeting with a card reader a few steps away.

Opening the heavy door, he held it with his foot and finally extended his hand out.

"My apologies. I am the excitable type. Werner Koeppel at your service."

Peter shook his hand and was impressed by the strength of his grip.

Werner then shook Nancy's hand. "Fraulein," he said as he held his grip just a bit longer.

Once they were finally in, Werner started his rapid-fire speech again. "Klaus has filled me in on most everything. Very disturbing and fascinating this business. Yes, very disturbing."

They continued down a sterile white hallway and passed the odd key card door as they walked along.

"My facility is at your disposal, young man. I have, at the end of the hallway, a team of specialists in medicine and computers awaiting your arrival. From what you requested through your e-mail, my kids, that is what I call my team," he said, "have put together a pretty spectacular program we can upload at anytime."

Werner stopped at the corridor's last door and swiped his entry card. Holding the door, the others entered Werner's lab. Nancy and Peter, now holding hands, stopped and took it all in. Looking to the left, they saw row upon row of computer servers in their own dedicated clean room. Peter panned right, seeing six ultra high-tech computer workstations, all manned by what looked like university students. They were all wearing glasses that reflected off their LCD screens in the darkened room. The area farther to the right looked like the medical set off a sci-fi movie. Three slabs extended out from the wall with large monitors above giving medical data. A cardiac crash cart was set off to the side along with other life sustaining equipment.

"No, I didn't put this all together just for you, my fine fellow," Werner chuckled at Peter, seeing his expression of awe. "This is the nerve center for my main business - medical bio feedback. I have over one million clients online worldwide." He dropped his voice a bit, "paying nineteen ninety-five a month, that log on each night…"

Peter went blank for a second and did the math. Sweet Jesus, that is twenty million a month, he thought. He got back into the conversation.

"…system automatically downloads new information and instructions to their laptops."

Nancy jumped in quickly as Werner took a breath, "So you have a million clients each night before bed downloading new info to do what?"

"Well my child, it is well known that the body uses electricity and is influenced by electrical impulses through the chakra points. Almost every ailment can be arrested and or cured by stimulating certain points on the body using different frequencies and lengths of time. Each night the clients have a laptop that we provide with a wireless interface that they place on their wrists and other points. Their laptop logs on to our servers," he pointed to the clean room on the left, "and accesses the new data for that client. The data collected from the last session is downloaded to the server, analyzed, and according to the program, adjustments are made for the next session. The new information is downloaded to the client's laptop through the Internet. It is all pretty automatic. Only a couple of steps for each client each night. It has to be personalized as we have every age and type of person imaginable online."

"But it works well?" Peter asked leadingly.

"Oh yes. The testimonials are amazing. People cured of non-curable diseases. Depressed to happy clients. It is truly amazing. Our business grew twenty-five percent last year on referrals alone."

"So," Werner continued as he walked towards the medical slabs, "enough of that. What we will be doing with this evening's download is adding an extra program that will give them a very happy dream. I'm even thinking of taking part in this session," he said with a big grin.

Nancy smiled to herself and asked, "Are you getting all one million on this tonight?"

"No. There are time zone differences, but they will

all be on within twelve hours or so. We also have filtered out the children from this and targeted only those from the demographic profiles who are over the age of eighteen."

Klaus came back to the group shaking his head, "I know why Fritz razed Beijing. I just checked the news reports and a Jack Montgomery was killed in a high-rise hotel there. Jack was the CEO of Zicon. I guess Fritz is trying to cover his ass. Funny thing, though, he did not die like the thousands that have so far. He was crushed to death in a stairwell right beside an emergency exit. Looks like a construction crew had toppled a wheelbarrow full of wet concrete on the other side of the exit door that afternoon and just left it for the morning crew to clean up. A hundred and fifty died in there with Jack."

"My God," Nancy said, covering her mouth. "How bad is it now?"

"It's Zurich times twenty, according to CNE News. Cities around the globe are in panic. Looting and rioting is happening everywhere and many are worried that this is the end of the world as we know it. If this keeps up, the world could literally burn in a few weeks."

Peter joined in, "A few weeks! Fritz did this in two nights. Tens of thousands are dead with billions in damage. One week of this and we will have anarchy. As long as his neg-hub keeps growing…and well, people need to sleep sometime. Nobody can stay awake for longer than seventy-two hours. This could be the end of…" He didn't finish.

CHAPTER THIRTY-THREE

The new team worked tirelessly for hours preparing and rechecking systems. In his role as father figure, Werner had insisted that they all stop and take time to eat at regular intervals. Time flew by as they went through the motions. At four in the morning, Peter was sitting upright on the middle of one of the medical slabs in the dreaming den. They had moved it to the center of the room so that all could get access to the slab. He was stripped to the waist, wearing only his jockeys.

As Nancy stood beside him attaching the endless rows of electrodes to his body, she felt a sexual tremor as her hand brushed along his thigh. She smiled as she saw his package jump a bit at her touch. She secretly wished they could sneak away for even a half an hour together to see if they would match sexually, but both Klaus and Werner drove them on. Nancy attached the final electrode, then gently pushed Peter down by his shoulders onto the slab in the center of the room so that he lay flat on his back. Peter stared upward only to be blinded by a large array of medical lights glaring down on him.

"Can we turn those off?" he said giving the lights a slight nod and pointing upward.

"Peter stop that!" Nancy held his arm down as the electrode wires dangled from it, "And yes, we will turn them off for you. Remember what I said about Christmas tree lights? Stay still. Actually I think we should strap you down this time."

She looked up from Peter then to Klaus and he nodded, standing across the other side of the slab. Peter reluctantly agreed.

It took a minute to secure the restraints and to jury rig one for his forehead. Peter now resembled a mental patient waiting to receive his prescribed electric shock treatment. The only difference was that these electrodes were meant to record his vitals and electrical patterns. He would be getting enough shock once he went into the dreamweave.

As luck would have it, Werner had built this part of the 'den' for easy clean up with a tiled floor slightly tilted to a drainage grate a few feet away. They had also installed a clear plastic wall perimeter twelve inches high around the slab, the purpose being to contain the mounds of ice that Werner had shipped in and stored in huge household freezers. If and when Peter hit Fritz's negative hub, they needed to keep him cool. Werner only hoped they had enough ice to do the job.

The electrodes had no charge. They only took readings from Peter so there was no chance of electrocution occurring, at least that is what they all hoped.

They had started the download a couple of hours ago at

2 AM local time to start building the positive dreamhub. It would not really kick into gear until 5 AM local time. This was the hour in which fifty percent of Werner's clients, on the east coast of North America would be affected. Dream time for millions was upon them.

Peter was already exhausted from lack of sleep and his mind raced away in the background. His tension was rising and he was still very fidgety in his restraints. They had shut off the lights above him, closed the blinds of the windows of the dreaming den and isolated him with only a glass door separating the medical lab from the computer room. In the darkened room, Peter was trying to force himself to sleep, but to no avail. He requested that there be no use of drugs as a relaxant so that his mental capacity stayed sharp. The onlookers peering through the glass doorway could not be heard but he sensed them; like a zebra at a watering hole sensing the lioness's hungry glare in the hidden tundra. By 5 A.M., he felt the pressure of time getting short and was getting irate with the situation.

Nancy turned to the others. "Ok now get going, he can tell we are here. Klaus, I don't care just go do something," she insisted after Klaus was about to say something.

Nancy walked into the room by herself. She closed the blinds that were hung on the door and then locked it. The room was very dark now. Only the glow of the monitors gave her light enough to see.

"Nancy?" Peter asked, looking up.

"Shhhh," she said softly, coming over to his side. "Relax, just relax and close your eyes. It's just you and I here, the rest have gone away," she said now gently patting his forehead. She continued stroking his head and started moving her hands slowly down his body to his chest, trying to avoid the wires. She continued downward, her hand lightly going over the bulge in his jockeys and he jolted.

"Relax," she said again, like a soothing nurse. Through the material she started stroking his bulge, as it started growing and twitching. She unbuttoned his jockeys and took his cock out, now rigid as a steel bar. Nancy slowly stroked up and down his shaft, always momentarily stopping at the tip, playing with it. Her other hand now cupped under his balls, slowly massaging them.

Peter was wriggling around, moaning lightly at finally enjoying the touch of his fantasy girl. Her fingertips were now almost not touching him, making her touch electrifying and then a hint of nothing.

Was this real? Peter thought. He hoped to god this was not a dream yet. He did not want to open his eyes and find out. The sensation of skin on skin jolted him again as Nancy's inner thigh rubbed his outer leg.

Nancy rested her hands on Peter's chest and finished getting over the small plastic perimeter. She sat back now on top of Peter, while his cock got caught up in her skirt.

Thank god I was wearing one, she thought.

Settling back she bunched up her skirt, her panties now exposed and settled down on his now throbbing cock. She moved back and forth, the material of the silk panties gliding over his length. Peter instinctively thrust his hips up in anticipation, his mind reeling in built-up sexual tension. Nancy kept this up for about five minutes letting the momentum of the strokes become faster, hearing Peter moan, waiting for the right moment. Suddenly she stopped and lifted her haunches up. Peter lifted his pelvis again, trying to connect. Only the touch of her inner thighs told him she was still there. Nancy shifted the material of the panties to one side exposing a now very wet inviting place. Desire that had been building and building finally took over as she reached down behind her, grabbed his cock, lifted it into place and then sat down letting it slip in right to the hilt.

Both Nancy and Peter's back arched simultaneously as guttural moans escaped, melding into one. Peter's eyes flew open for a mere second only to find Nancy's laser stare into his. He closed his eyes again as she started a rhythmic movement up and down his shaft. The restraints drove his lust even further and he could only thrust upwards in response. Nancy now had her hands back on his chest, her hips pumping up and down, twisting right and left. Her love for Peter was now apparent as she continued on. Peter was in ecstasy as his girl picked up the pace.

His mind swam in a multi-colored swirl, as Nancy's thrusts grew harder, faster and deeper. Nancy grunted as Peter now started matching her, his cock going deeper still with each stroke. The final build of passion began as the two were now one. Their bodies responded to the pitch of movement, which was now intense. The slab began to shake as Nancy and Peter were now a machine. It started in Nancy first. The edge of climax teasingly there, taunting her to release. Peter sensed it as she pushed against his cock from the inside and he thrust even harder as the restraints dug into this wrists, arms and legs. Nancy's eyes flew open upon the thrust of the waves coming so, so close. She continued pumping as fast as she could. Suddenly it was there, that sweet sensation that she was going over the edge. She pumped two more times, sat up and then put her full weight onto his cock. It slipped in as far as it had ever been, then it began.

Peter knew she was there by her movements. Even though it was their first time, she was already a knowing lover. He had been ready to explode for what seemed like an hour, holding back for her, his love. He lost it when she sat down on him that final time. Her tight walls gripped his cock and pulsated as she went off.

The sound of a long groan came to his ears as his cock released spasming deep inside her heavenly warmth. His mind tumbled backwards as Nancy squeezed his cock from within and then cupped his balls from behind. The scream of ecstasy was now his as his cock shot and shot. Nancy, still quivering from the constant waves, then moved her head down towards his and said, "I love you, Peter Sutherland." And before he could answer, placed her open mouth over his, thrusting in her tongue.

Peter was fully relaxed as this angel gave him a long delicious kiss while they were still coupled together. He did not move. This couldn't be real as he drifted backwards, backward from this reality. Only an echo remained, "I love you Peter, Peter…Peter…"

CHAPTER THIRTY-FOUR

Peter lay on his back. "Nancy, I love you," he said.

Peter opened his eyes only to see blue. He flailed for a moment when he realized that nothing was supporting his back. He flipped over and the sight of the ground thousands of feet below him gave him a fright.

Ok, now I'm dreaming, he thought, and he wasn't falling. He simply floated there watching the small puffy clouds go by. He thought of Nancy for a bit and her magic to get him to finally relax.

Near the horizon Peter saw something very green and large. Even before he realized it, he was heading in that direction, sort of like flying. As he approached, the green shimmered like glittering jewels. On closer approach, he saw that the green was actually a huge forest of thousand foot high trees. The whole canopy was busy with winged fairies, he assumed, very beautiful naked fairies. Guilt flashed in his mind as he stared at them, "It's only a dream," he said out loud, his commitment to Nancy already taking hold. Two extremely sexy nymphs or fairies came up to him. Their slender perfect bodies brought another rise to his friend below. Down boy, he thought, I am here to work.

Each took a hand and led him toward an even taller clump of trees, towering over the rest of the forest. An entrance to a stairway appeared within and the fairies floated him to the landing deck. He felt his bare feet touch the wooden planks. The fairies giggled and then flew away. Peter looked down and noticed that his clothing was the same as in reality, his jockeys still on. He was glad about that. Funny to be self-conscious in your own dream, or was it his own dream now? He looked around again. The entrance was even higher than the other treetops, with dozens of fairies flitting around. Peter saw a handrail, took a hold of it and started his descent.

Quickly, the scene changed from brightness to a closed in but still comfortable feel. Peter walked down three flights through the large, thick foliage. After a few more flights of stairs, the canopy opened up and Peter came to a larger landing overlooking the space below. He went up to the railing and stared down in awe. The sound of music was everywhere. The electronic tribal beat was almost hypnotizing and Peter caught himself swaying with the music. The diffused light from above gave it a dreamy feeling. And the view: endless trees with stairways all heading down to a huge centre walkway far, far down. The fairies were also down there. Their glowing wings providing a reference point as to how large this area was.

Peter proceeded down, stopping now and then to take

another look. The music grew louder as he descended. He came to another landing and was startled to see three bodies on a bed of leaves, slowly caressing themselves. Peter smiled as he passed by, even as the one woman tried to pull Peter into their playpen. Peter continued down, amazed at the openness and caring that he saw in other groups all just caressing each other.

Still very high up in the trees, he finally reached the immense platform he had seen from way above. Suspended in the air, he saw what looked like several thousand people milling around, touching each other as they walked by. Peter saw an opening in the trees and slowly walked toward it, now fully erect again as he was fondled generously from time to time.

Bright sunshine blinded him briefly as he emerged from the trees. The wood platform had now changed to stone tiles, which Peter followed through the crowd. He started getting worried that he may not find a way out of what must be Werner's positive dreamhub. Oh what wet dreams the world will be having tonight, he thought.

The crowd ahead started dissipating. He found himself on a gigantic stone arched staircase that wrapped around in a semi-circle for what looked like a half of a mile. Peter thought it was more like a 'stairwall'; it was so immense. The steps down, all two hundred or so, funneled to a central Roman looking plaza at the bottom, stretching for a square mile. It looked as if this was the end of the line. It was Vegas on steroids filled with plazas, pools and lounging areas. Peter stopped to take it all in, only to be gently pushed forward by the now growing masses behind him. As he went down the stairs he noticed that the crowd's clothing had changed to white cloths held together by gold braids or jewelry. Also, the scent of sexual awareness was everywhere.

Wow, what a program Werner's kids had put together, he thought. For the next while, Peter walked around more dazed than anything. His own sexual desires growing again as the sounds of laughter and sexual foreplay joined the visual feast. Something did not gel though as he thought that everyone gathered here was too perfect, not one unattractive participant in sight. A tall seductive brunette crossed his path and without hesitation, wrapped her arms around him and started French kissing him. Her tongue meshed with his as he felt her reach down to his cock.

Tongue? He broke away and looked at her. She smiled and then kept going. Again his mind whirled at the whole magnitude of this scenario. Over a hundred thousand must be in this positive dreamhub. His mind swung back to the task at hand. He started concentrating on how to find a way out of this hub, to break free and find Fritz's neg-hub. He filled his thoughts with negative images, the fire lions, Tony's burning room, and images from the news services.

A glint of sunlight in the distance brought his attention to an area not yet too populated. Walking in that direction, he was again mesmerized by the sheer beauty of this dreamhub. He passed dozens of group-sized hot tubs all just a bit different, mostly in a Roman or Greek theme, with columns and loose fabrics blowing in the wind. Most were empty at the moment as the crowds had not filed in behind him yet. The party has just begun, he surmised as the glint of sunlight caught his eyes again and he renewed his quest with an increasing pace. Coming up to several mirrors he saw reflected back hundreds, maybe thousands coming down the grand stairwall heading for the acres and acres of pleasure pits and hot tubs. Whoa, was his only thought. He looked back toward the mirrors and walked into the midst of them.

The gold trimmed elaborate mirrors formed a small hemisphere, as if you were to look at a newly tailored suit at a tailor's shop. Peter stepped up to them and was shocked to see himself reflected back as a Roman Centurion. The epitome of a handsome Roman warrior was what the mirrors portrayed him as.

"Everyone has a mirror image here. A golden image of themselves," he said to himself out loud. He stood there for a while looking at his alter ago only to become hot from the reflection of the sun off the mirrors. As he started moving, the mirrors shifted with him, the sun's heat now intensifying. He moved further still only to run into another bank of mirrors. He quickly turned around and now found himself surrounded by them. He could see and hear the crowds through gaps in the mirrors but could not get through.

Ok, Peter thought, this is my way out of this paradise. But how? The reflection was now blinding. Peter squinted and tried to shade his eyes. The heat felt like a blue flame. Unable to see now, Peter stumbled around coming in contact with one of the mirror panels. He jumped back as his hand was singed. His heel caught an edge and he started falling backwards. He fell backwards into a small circular pool that had materialized out of nowhere. There was instant relief from the heat. He opened his eyes to see blue water above him with the sun's reflection now heating the water. Peter flipped over and dove down as the light from the reflection above faded.

Volumes of water fell onto the tiled floor as it drained from the medical slab.

"False alarm," Klaus said as he looked at the now normalized readings on a monitor.

"I wouldn't say that," Nancy said worryingly, as she pointed to a large blister on Peter's right shoulder blade. "I wouldn't say that at all."

CHAPTER THIRTY-FIVE

Peter's dreamline shot out of the artificial positive dreamhub like a comet shooting around the sun. It's exiting point now different from the entry vector. As it pulled away Peter saw that the positive hub, circling in a clockwise motion, had grown to about forty percent of Fritz's hub which he saw in the distance. Tens of thousands of dreamlines circled the positive hub, being attracted to it. It would be a major force in the dreamweave soon. Peter's dreamline faded away in the distance, now just a speck of light.

His dreamline was being drawn in by the more powerful dreamhub. As his line zipped toward Fritz's neg-hub, the dreamweave space around him became more congested as thousands of dreamlines also headed toward the neg-hub. These dreamlines were like in a horse race, jostling for position, bumping into each other, crossing and also mixing at times.

Peter had washed up on a sandy beach. He was propped up against a palm tree wearing his now wet jockeys again.

He could feel the grating of sand was in body parts where it shouldn't be and he spent a few moments wiping it away. A small mongrel of a dog skirted past, sniffing at everything, keeping a wary eye on Peter as it kept walking on along the beach. The dog was fifty feet away when Peter heard it yelp. Looking up, he saw the dog being attacked by long slender tentacles coming up from the sand. They were trying to capture the dog by wrapping around it. The dog proved to be too quick, zigging and zagging, it's slippery coat making it hard to hold on to. The dog headed back toward Peter with a pleading and desperate look on its face. Peter got up quickly as he saw the tentacles popping up behind the dog. He turned around and was faced with thick jungle terrain. He wasted no time jumping into the foliage. About a hundred feet in he looked back, the beach and dog were gone.

"Ok, where I am being pushed to this time?" he said loudly just to hear his own voice. He suddenly heard the crack of a whip beyond the foliage in front of him. He squatted quickly and placed a hand over his mouth to stifle the sound. Now on his hands and knees trying to brush away the ferns in his face, he crawled up to the line of bushes that bordered a path.

Peter heard a louder crack followed by a strangled wail just as he moved some branches from his hiding spot. The scene was out of this world. "Well look where I am," he said to himself quietly. Ragged prisoners were being herded by large muscle-bound guards sheathed in leather straps. The guards were dog-faced like German Shepherds.

Each brandished what looked like a whip, but the actual whip portion was a ribbon of fire as thick as a regular whip, ending with a black handle. The guards certainly used them like whips, snapping them in the air, shards of flame escaping at each crack. They were herding the endless stream of prisoners; many almost crawling from the injuries inflicted.

A prisoner broke from the ranks for a moment, only to be whipped relentlessly by the guard nearby. Each strike was followed by the sound of searing flesh and the howl of agony. The man fell to his knees from the onslaught. Another guard joined in, both laughing in a barkish manner, their jaws snapping as they rained the blows down on the melting form. The form, now silent, simply melted into the dirt path. Prisoners walked over it without even a thought.

Searing pain exploded in Peter's head as he felt his back racked with a fire whip. He instinctively moved away to the left only to be whipped by another. The only way was forward through the bushes, only to be whipped on his side by a guard on the path, herding him towards the right to join the march with the others.

Should have known they would patrol the sides, he concluded as the pain ebbed from him. "Damn Tony, where are you?" he said under his breath. Another lash tip hit his right calf. Howling, he smelled the burnt flesh now in his nostrils.

"Nof Tokof!" the guard snarled at him.

Fuck, ok there, Rin Tin Tin! he yelled in his mind. He now limped along with the others.

Hours passed as they drudged along what seemed like an endless path through the jungle, garnering many more welts from his pleasant captors along the way.

Peter started a conversation with himself; Just excellent dude, this is fun. Walking with Spot and the boys for hours. Well what are hours here in Dreamland anyway? I could be in paradise valley with my own harem right now, but no, Peter has to save the fucking planet. Tony is not showing up, Fritz's neg-hub looks like it has grown, probably too strong to break into from *Here*. Face it old buddy, you are supposed to be a clever one, think it out.

He shuffled along, his mind now feverishly churning, analyzing, and calculating. It didn't take too long to figure out what his strategy would be. He would have to die. It was the only way out of the neg-hub to get to *Here*. A strange calm came over Peter as the decision was made but also trepidation that he would not be in Nancy's arms again. As the previous hours had passed, he had witnessed hundreds of executions by the guards unleashing their tirades with the fire-whips. They had all died horribly and melted into the dirt. Wasting no more time, Peter stepped out of line and faced the nearest guard.

"Hey dog breath!" he yelled and ran to tackle the behemoth. He actually surprised the guard who had not drawn back the whip. Hitting him full force, he was shocked to find that the guard was not as heavy as he appeared. The whip had been thrown to the side and now the jaws of the guard started snapping at his face. For a moment he thought that he might actually win against his opponent when the rain of fire engulfed him. Five guards threw everything they had into punishing Peter. The pain quickly became a numb feeling as the stench of his burnt flesh filled his nostrils. The smell was mixed with something else - burnt fur. His opponent was under the same lashes, howling as much as Peter. Both had separated, both in agony. Spasms and blinding light now took over Peter's vision. Searing tracks crisscrossed his body as he rolled around trying to protect himself. Blinded now, the lashes felt like fire raining from the sky. Peter's flesh felt as though it was melted like metal before being poured as an ingot.

Pain no longer registered, only the surreal feeling of liquidness. Peter started drifting.

Drifting from what to what? he thought. Best drugs I have ever been on, he countered. The sensation of floating and sinking at the same time challenged his senses.

Instantly Peter was in complete darkness. He felt that he still had eyes and instinctively opened them. Fritz's neg-hub sat there in his view. It was huge, spinning counter-clockwise, brilliant against the darkness. As he was receding from it along its side, he could notice his own dreamline pulling away. As he drifted further away, the scope and size of Fritz's dream hub amazed him. It still took up a large portion of his view, but off to the left another large hub came into view. It spun clockwise and rivaled Fritz's in size.

My positive dreamhub, he surmised as he started to

look around.

"You are not supposed to be in *Here*," greeted a beautiful being.

"Took you long enough," Tony quipped.

Peter looked into his friend's eyes, "So I really am here."

Tony spread his arms showing him the view from the balcony, "*Here* is where it's at."

CHAPTER THIRTY-SIX

"Jesus! More ice, we're losing him!" came the shrill from Nancy. Buckets of big cubed ice cascaded down over Peter, the steam rising instantly. A monitor on the side that gave his internal and external skin temperature read:

Internal	42 C / 109 F
Exterior skin	57 C / 135 F

Peter, other than for the close call earlier, had been stable for two hours, his vitals normal for deep sleep. Then just minutes ago it had started with a huge scream and Peter arching his back testing the restraints. Peter was in agony as welts appeared on his body. Many tears were falling from Nancy's cheeks as she tried to keep him alive.

Werner muscled his way to Peter's side, quickly looking over the monitors. His vast medical knowledge and experience kicking into high gear.

"Everybody stop!" he yelled out, then in German, "Schnell!"

Everyone complied except for Nancy. Werner, with his surprising strength, grabbed and pulled her back.

"We have to let it run its course," he said sympathetically

and also authoritatively.

"Bullshit!" she yelled spinning around to release his grip, "Yes he will die, but on my terms, not as a flame thrower. I have seen the pictures of the charred corpses."

Everyone stared at her. Peter and the equipment making the only sounds in the room.

"Now! You bastards, keep him cool!" she yelled again from her diaphragm.

They all awoke from the trance they were in and got back to work, even Werner. They fought on, Peter withering on the slab. A constant rain now fell to the tile floor below from the melted ice.

"Nancy!" an eerie voice came from Peter as all the monitors started wailing in alarms. Nancy grabbed his hand, only to repel from the heat. The EKG monitor was completely erratic and then suddenly flat lined and the sound of a constant beep of death filled the air. Peter settled back on the slab in a wet splat, the steam almost over taking them all, his body horribly disfigured with welts and burns.

"Now we wait," she sighed.

"Not long, my dear. Not long." Werner chipped in quickly.

Within forty-five seconds they were working on Peter again, this time to bring him back from the other side.

Peter was now stable again, as stable as he could be, but not conscious.

"I don't know if he is in a coma or if he is still caught

up in his dreams," Werner mentioned. Nancy still had tear-streaked cheeks but was now a bit more relaxed since Peter was back. One of Werner's staff came into the dreaming den and whispered to Werner.

"Ja, Ja, danke," he said. The messenger left them. "We now have sixty percent of our members in the dream scenario. That is probably the most we will get because of the time differences."

"Six hundred thousand," Klaus whistled. "What a party that has to be."

Standing on the balcony overlooking *Here*, Peter, Tony and the Being were looking out toward the horizon.

"Peter, I tell you, *Here* is smaller since I arrived but the concept of time is really tricky."

Peter nodded, "So that blackness which is the horizon is now getting closer?"

"Yes, almost every time I look out I can see changes. Just look at the streets. They are more crowded as everyone is getting squeezed back. Someone just told me that being beside the blackness is like, well...hmm, like nothing. No feelings or emotions, just emptiness."

"Death," Peter answered.

"Yes, death," the Being answered. "Which you had been but are not now. This is why you must leave *Here*. Your presence is increasing the blackness. You are not of *Here*. You must go back."

"So, I am still alive?"

"Yes, you lived again just as you entered *Here*."

"You could sense that?"

"My bracelet became darker."

Both Tony and Peter quickly moved their eyesight to the large heavily tarnished bracelet on the wrist of the Being.

Tony started in, "Come again? Your bracelet turned darker?"

"Yes, it has changed color since the clothing of the, what do you call them?"

"The Nazis," Tony answered.

"Yes, since the Nazis began coming to *Here*"

"Is this bracelet part of your power?" Peter asked.

"I have no power. I am just *Here* as you are."

"Can I take a look at that?" Tony asked.

The Being looked at Tony for a couple of moments, almost like weighing a major decision and then looked over at Peter. He simply nodded. The Being, taking Peter's nod as her confirmation, removed the bracelet and handed it to Tony in that way that was of the Being. As soon as the Being's fingers left the bracelet it changed to brilliant gold. Both men jumped a bit.

"Holy shit!" Peter exclaimed.

"You might be right about that," Tony answered back. "Solid gold, judging from the weight. But gold does not tarnish."

"I thought it would be copper or brass from the look of it," Peter held out his hand to take it. They both jumped again as the bracelet turned back to the darker greenish color as it touched Peter's fingers. Tony never said anything, but his eyes expressed a million questions.

"Don't know," Peter said shaking his head, "Don't know."

"It's your talisman," a raised voice said from a few feet away.

"My what?" Peter queried.

Manuel walked over almost too relaxed, "Its your talisman, young man. As the Being stated, you are not supposed to be here. But your presence is most probably the single most important event to *Here*."

Tony nodded slowly while thinking and then said, "He has to take it back with him."

"Yes Tony," Manuel shifted toward him, "A talisman is an important object that is brought back from the afterlife. My ancestors talked of such things through their tales. Ancient tales of civilizations more grand than ours."

No one said anything. The sound of *Here* buzzed around them. Peter started to turn. "You must take this bracelet from *Here*," the Being stated, not asking.

"Take it where?" he asked, hefting the weight in his hand.

"Back to where you started."

"You must save us," Manuel said closing his eyes and nodding like in a prayer, "You must get back or all of *Here* will be gone."

CHAPTER THIRTY-SEVEN

The four looked out at the blackness that was now visibly moving inward to *Here*.

Tony took Peter's arm, "Come on Pete, you've got to leave now." Peter hesitated as visions of fire-whips took control.

"Now! I don't want to know what happens when the blackness takes all of *Here*." Tony had a pleading look in his eyes.

Peter looked at the bracelet in his hand and then up to the Being still floating above the tile. He lifted the bracelet a bit with his hand toward the Being as an unspoken thank you. The Being smiled back.

Within a flash, Tony and Peter were back in the dream weave, riding on top of a dreamline. Peter had the mild sensation of being part of a roaring '20's flapper party.

Tony looked over at Peter. "Good dream this guy is having," he said as he looked down toward the dreamline.

Peter smirked and looked out. The dreamweave was abuzz. Lines were shooting from everywhere all heading in one direction. Off to the distance two huge dreamhubs were heading toward each other.

"This is as far as I can go my friend," Tony said with sadness.

"Yes, friends even in the afterlife. I will try my damndest to get back."

"No pressure, but the world and this afterlife is kind of in the balance."

"Always the optimist," Peter chuckled. He looked back at the hubs, which now looked like they were going to collide soon.

"Aw shit. I am going to have to go through some of Fritz's..." he turned toward Tony, but Tony was gone. Despair engulfed Peter as he now hurtled toward the hubs, which had both stopped spinning in their opposite positions.

Riding on top of the dreamline, he watched the hubs close in. The power of each hub was almost matched. The centrifugal force of each one negated the spin of the other. Peter had no reference points to judge the distance between them, but they would crash into each other in mere moments. Peter was awestruck at the visuals hitting his retinas at that moment. They were like two immense spheres that shimmered with countless bright flashes, like flashbulbs going off at a darkened concert hall. They were surrounded by hundreds of thousands of dreamlines being drawn in from every direction. The dreamweave was converging at this point and time. The dreams of the world were now being held hostage to both artificial dreamhubs.

His eyes registered that they were to collide. Just as

the two dreamhubs slammed into each other, an extremely powerful energy wave shot out and hit Peter. Although not possible, he felt as he would almost fall off the dreamline he was riding. Powerful aftershock energy waves came across him as he tried to regain his focus.

Shit, *Here* is going to get pummeled, he thought as his eyes were blinded by the light that emanated from the joining of the two hubs.

Simultaneously, all the converging dreamlines now shifted their heading toward the joined spot of the two hubs. Peter shuddered as he thought of what awaited him. He grabbed the bracelet tighter in his hand then tried to fit it over his left hand only to get stuck at the knuckles. He looked up. His dreamline, which felt like the flapper party was now in full swing, was on its final leg to meld into the now forged hubs. With an uncountable number of dreamlines all racing toward the center, Peter placed a death grip on the bracelet and rode into the fray.

"He must be heading back," Klaus yelled as Peter's vitals started to elevate.

"So soon?" Nancy said remorsefully. She did not want to see Peter in that state again as his injuries would take weeks to heal already.

"Clash of the Titans!" Werner said in a knowing voice as he stormed into the dreaming den. "Peter's predictions are coming true, I think," he was nodding his head. "Feedback from the online members is outstanding. Anxiety levels have jumped twenty percent in the last few minutes. Something is influencing the positive dreamhub. We have uploaded a counteractive program that should help within a few minutes to calm everyone down. I hope."

Peter materialized into the middle of complete confusion and panic. It took him a few seconds to grasp his environment. Again, the Roman baths surrounded him.

He looked around and could almost not comprehend the scene. Thousands of Roman hot tubs, baths and pillowed areas now took over vast areas. The stairwall was still there, much larger, but the traffic on it was light, not like before. Everyone must be busy, he thought. At least I landed in the positive hub.

The baths were full of naked bodies. Some baths in full orgies with sounds of moaning and laughter battling now with the increasing sounds of screaming and running feet from his right. A bug buzzed by his ear and he swatted at it. "Shit!" he said as he grabbed his scorched hand dropping the bracelet. He stooped quickly and picked it up, and while straightening he looked at the burnt welt on the back of his right hand. He looked over his right shoulder and saw dozens of flying insects lit up like large fireflies.

"Those aren't fireflies," he said to no one as he turned and started jogging with the now fleeing crowd. Multiple screams had him turn around to look. A bath full of partiers were swatting at some of the firebugs only to find out that swatting them was not the safe thing to do. The swatting just aggravated the firebugs and began drawing more of them. Peter half turned to jog again when he saw a lit stream coming from the negative hub's direction. Hundreds of firebugs in a fine stream wove through the air like a string of fire. The fire string approached the bath of swatting partiers. In a flash the fire string homed in and started circling above the bath, hesitating for a second, and then diving straight down into the water. The screams turned to shrills as the fire string of hundreds continued to dive in as their heat added to the already hot water. The string finally ended, but the damage was done as the water began to boil. The firebugs were still lit underneath which made an eerie glow. The poor partiers who were now parboiled sat in deathly silence in the bath.

Peter turned his jog into a run toward the stairwall, more frightened that he had ever been. By now, on each side of him, the firebugs buzzed around as he dodged over baths, furniture and stumbled people.

It took him much longer to get back to the stairwall this time. The positive dreamhub had expanded exponentially with the influx of new dreamers that had been added in the last few hours. Finally reaching the base, he took a breath and stared up at the now daunting stairwall that had increased in height. It could be compared to the size of the great pyramid of Giza. Peter took in a huge breath and started up the stairwall. After pounding up the stairs two at a time, it didn't take long for him to power out.

He stopped and looked up. "Shit, only a quarter of the way up," he said in a jagged breath, hunched over with his hands resting on his knees. Straightening up in a bit of a stretch, he turned around to look over the pleasure plaza. He first looked down the stairwall and out trying to see how far he was or not from the firebug's infestation. He was amazed to see that he had outrun them and that at the moment they were content on terrorizing the baths and pools about half a mile away. He looked even further back and was mesmerized by the scene. On the horizon, large black clouds were slowly encroaching on the sunny paradise. It definitely looked as though Fritz's neg-hub was still stronger than this positive one.

As the clouds gathered, he moved his eyes from the horizon back to the ground and was startled. A column of ground-hovering open troop transports emerged from the cloudbank. The transports were loaded with the dog-faced guards who had killed him. That took a second or two for Peter to absorb. He looked back again. The transports began unloading the 'canine storm troopers', as Peter called them and took over where the firebugs had started. Even from the distance, Peter could still hear the screams and shrieks as the fire whips began to rain blows now in full force. The storm troopers started advancing on the fleeing crowd with more hover transports materializing from the neg-hub side to support the advance.

Peter was about to turn and continue on up the stairwall when he saw at the center of the attack a small side battle start as Roman Centurions, as he had once been dressed, start a counterattack on the canine storm troopers. Peter silently cheered the Centurions on as they fought broadsword to fire whips and actually started to gain some ground. More Centurions joined in from the plaza as they saw the counter attack. Peter actually began to feel that the positive hub might be able to repel the neg-hub. The battle appeared to be turning to the favor of the Centurions as they used the famous Roman V attack formation, with their shields driving a wedge into the canine storm troopers. The fire whips were now just bouncing off the shields and the Centurion's swords were now felling storm troopers.

Peter's anxiety peaked though as several dozen lion torches broached the cloud mass and descended toward the ensuing battle. Peter could already see the writing on the wall as the lion torches acted like air support to ground troops. The Centurions didn't have a chance. He turned and started scaling the now even taller stairwall with renewed vigor.

Almost breathless, he stopped at the top of the stairs and turned back to take a quick scan of his situation.

From his high vantage point, he now had a broad-scope view of what was really happening down below. Fritz's minions from the neg-hub had formed a so-called army and were steadily advancing. The firebugs were the advance shock troops swooping in far ahead of the rest, causing panic and their own share of terror. The battle behind the firebugs had grown even although the lion torches had joined the fight. It seemed as though more and more people had stopped fleeing and joined in the battle, only to be repelled when a lion torch or two moved into the fray. Peter nodded his head in confirmation to himself at the thought that the neg-hub was stronger and would ultimately overtake this positive hub. He was the only hope left to bring the talisman back through this hub to his reality. As Manuel had told him just before he left, the power of the

talisman, the bracelet in his hand, could be the only thing
to stop both artificial dreamhubs once and for all. He had
been rushed to leave *Here* and had only caught parts of the
tail-end of what Manuel was trying to get at. Just as they
had left he heard, "The key to the dreamweave," and "Not
to fall into the wrong hand."

He added pressure to his grip of the bracelet as he saw
that the firebugs were staying more on the lower levels for
now. Peter turned and headed toward the treed area.

"Thank you, Werner, for keeping this party going," he
said as he started jogging again.

Now on the walkway from the stairs, the full magnitude
of how large this dreamhub had grown filled his vision.
What had taken him a few dozen feet to cross before was
now a major jog back to the treed area. While he jogged
at a fast pace, he tried to look up and see the tops of the
trees ahead and almost stumbled since he had to look so far
up. He was coming up to the entrance of the platform area
and sprinted the last hundred feet. He entered the platform
under the trees and was dumbfounded by their sheer height
from ground level. "Shit, they must be sixty to seventy
stories tall," he said discouragingly, knowing that he had
to climb the next stairway.

The brightness now changed to a diffused serene
light as the sound of sensual, up-tempo house music now
enfolded him. Raised mats littered the platform area, all
occupied by naked participants.

Whoa, this has gotten more interesting, he thought. He

started weaving through the mats toward the main stairwell as hands lightly caressed or enticed him to join them. The sexual energy was intense now, much more then when he had been here before.

A hand gripped his ankle as he was trying to skirt by a large matted area. He had no choice as he was dragged into the mêlée that ensued. Hands, soft hands, started caressing him all over as he tried to get himself back toward the edge of the mat. Peter, now on his back, was trying to keep his composure. It was very difficult with hands roaming over everything and sounds of moans and the scent of sex mere inches from him. The more he tried to wriggle free, the more tightly gripped he found himself. A well-toned mulatto woman ripped his shorts down and Peter gasped as she swallowed his cock whole. A pert breast with saucer nipples from another participant was pushed into his face as the temptress below gained speed.

Meanwhile, back in the lab, everyone became quiet and averted each other's eyes as they saw Peter's penis jump to full attention and begin to throb.

Nancy said in a low voice to herself, "Enjoy it baby, you deserve it."

CHAPTER THIRTY-EIGHT

The rhythm was too much. The sensations were
overpowering. Still unable to detach himself from the orgy
pit and the temptress who was performing incredible feats
with her tongue, the build up took over and Peter screamed
in release. The temptress swallowed every drop and didn't
let go of her prize. She just kept on going. Peter was in
tremors when fingers tried to wrench the bracelet from his
still clenched left hand. That alone broke his spell as his
resolve came flooding back to his core. He brushed off the
intruding fingers and pushed off the now crazed temptress
who took it in stride, grabbing hold of another cock within
seconds.

Dragging himself off the mat, he rolled onto the
platform with his shorts still looped around his ankles.
Another hand tried for his foot and he sidestepped it,
jumping on one leg trying to get his shorts up. Looking
back toward the stairwall he saw that a few firebugs had
now flown over the edge.

No time to dawdle, he surmised. He now sprinted
toward the staircase he had come down. Running was

difficult as bodies sprawled everywhere. The treed area now held a hundredfold more people than when he had arrived. Hundreds of thousands, maybe a million were in states of ecstasy for as far as the eye could see.

The air, if there was any air left, he thought, was electrified with the most intense sexual energy that had ever existed. Not surprisingly, he still was running along with his cock at full attention. As he approached the first landing to the towering staircase, familiar sounds of panic began ringing through the tree city. Spurred on by the same panic, Peter didn't waste any time as he started running up the flights.

At the twentieth landing, Peter was totally out of breath. "Ok," he was doubled over with his hands on his knees, "how in the hell can I be tired running in a dream?" he said to no one. He looked over the edge and a sense of foreboding came over him. Twenty percent of the tree city was in turmoil, the firebugs going about their deadly business.

"Fuck Me," came out of Peter's mouth as he witnessed the next horror coming through the treed entrance, a full battalion of canine storm troopers riding on top of lion torches. The pairs floated in, the storm troopers lashing out with their lethal fire whips at the intertwined bodies lying on the mats, still completely oblivious of their surroundings. Thousands of firebugs also flowed through with the now mounted cavalry. Some of the mounted lion torches began to break away and started rising. One headed toward his staircase. Peter pushed away from the rail. Shaking his head, he looked up to the stairway and saw no end in sight. "Aghhh!" was his only response as he attacked the staircase again.

Rounding another flight he reached what he guessed was the fiftieth landing.

"Fresh meat!" said a very burly naked bald man blocking the landing. Peter didn't even think as he charged the mountainous man, coming in low and taking out his knees like a line backer. The man buckled and fell down the stairs behind Peter.

Yells of "Hey stop!" fell to his ears, as he kept on climbing, his legs and arms now in a relentless motion. Pounding up a flight, grabbing the railing to spin, pounding up again two steps at a time, and running across the landing to the next flight. He did it again and again. Reaching the seventieth flight, he had to stop again for to catch his breath, taking precious seconds to look over the railing. The bottom was a madhouse; sex was not the motivation now as self-preservation had taken hold. Thousands surged in various directions trying to escape the fires started in the trees by the firebugs.

He looked across and saw four lion torches with canine storm troopers ascending toward him. The heat intensity of the lions made the branches ignite as they passed by the trees.

The whole tree city was quickly becoming an inferno.

He could hear the pounding of footsteps and he looked straight down to see that thirty flights below a string of naked hysterical forms were coming up fast.

Peter looked up to see about twenty or so more flights to go and then finally, also bright light. Now that he had the goal in view, he increased his pace as the reflections of the lower fires bounced on the foliage above him.

For the final five flights, Peter had blanked out everything - all of the screams, the crackling of the fires and the pounding of hundreds on the staircases. Just his breath, his footfalls and inner voice urged him on. At the top landing he looked over one last time. Being too high, all he saw were masses moving back and forth, squirming in the intense heat from the fires.

Those damn lions are getting too close, he thought as they had reached around the seventieth floor by now. Again, he took a quick peek down the staircase and saw a lone escapee down ten or so flights with a pack following close by. Almost there, he thought, proud of himself, running up the final flight to come up above the canopy landing, which was still serene, lush and green. Keeping his momentum going, desperately still clutching the gold bracelet, he did a bit of a jump and started flying away from the landing and heading back toward reality.

"Well he has stopped twitching and his heart rate is back to normal," Werner said nodding his head. They surrounded Peter and the clear plastic enclosure. Peter was glistening in sweat from what they did not know, but at least he was not burning up. They had dozens of bags of ice at the ready. They even had brought in a couple of burn treatment nurses, which made the room even more crowded.

"He is calm now, like he is floating," quipped Klaus.

Nancy stood by his side holding his hand and started up, "Peter? Peter, I am here Peter. Wake up, it's over baby." She clenched his hand. Peter trembled.

"I think he is coming out of it," Werner said excitedly. Everyone took a step back and audible gasps came from all as a shimmering glow began to appear. Even Nancy joined them as Peter began to almost pulse back and forth, from flesh and bone to translucent.

It was one of the nurses on the opposite side of the slab that yelled out and pointed, "His hand. Look at his left hand!"

Nancy looked down to the hand that she had just been holding and was mesmerized to see a tarnished bracelet being tightly clenched by her man. Peter continued pulsing. The translucent stage was getting shorter. His real self was becoming more and more visible as the glow started to recede.

Nancy reached over to take the bracelet and, as she touched it, Peter pulsed one more time and stopped. Peter now just lay as still as before it all began.

"It's gone," the nurse said now, "The bracelet is gone!"

CHAPTER THIRTY-NINE

Peter was heading backwards struggling as he screamed, "No, let me go!"

"Welcome," was the response from the two lithe fairies that had Peter by the arms, gliding him back to the canopy landing. Reasoning with them was hopeless as he knew they were just part of the dream. Think damn it, was his only thought, now totally frustrated.

They delivered him upon the landing. Peter's feet were now back on the smooth wood floor. The fairies released him and they headed toward the staircase saying, "Join us."

Peter was about to respond when the lead escapee he had seen earlier came up the steps almost running into the fairies. Peter stared at the three who were looking at each other for a blink or two and then they began convulsing in unison. Firebugs had been chasing the lead escapee up the staircase and they didn't stop. Like bullets going through two or more bodies, the firebugs pierced through the torso, leg and neck of the lead guy. Each piercing was like a small charred hole that let you see clear through the body.

They went through him first and then straight through the two fairies who were pierced several times as the firebugs looped back and re-entered the fairies again, heading back toward the escapee.

Time stood still as Peter took this all in, standing twenty-odd feet away. In actuality only two seconds went passed as Peter took another second to turn and jump out again to escape.

Manuel, Tony and the Being were crowded together on the balcony. The thousands upon thousands of frightened arrivals to *Here* now occupied every inch of spare room. The Being looked out toward the blackness which now surrounded the four-block radius that *Here* had now squeezed into.

"Come on buddy," Tony mumbled. The Being merely smiled at him.

"He is at it again folks!" Werner yelled out as Peter began to pulse again. The health monitors took on an eerie dance. As each translucent phase occurred, the monitors would simply die and then resurrect themselves again when Peter materialized.

All eyes were now on the left hand. The bracelet was clearly there. With each pulse it became more solid. The pulses came quicker and quicker. Peter's eyes started to flutter. Nancy reached over again and neared the bracelet. The pulsing came to a fever pitch. The monitors now started to smoke and arc electrically from the relentless rhythm.

As Nancy grabbed the bracelet still clenched in his hand, Peter's eyes flew open. Both sets of eyes pierced into each other. A start of a smirk came across his face. A final pulse made him arch his back and then he screamed.

The room exploded into pandemonium as five firebugs appeared from Peter, the charred holes showing through to the medical slab underneath him. The firebugs started buzzing around as everyone tried to swat at them.

Nancy would not let go of the bracelet in Peter's clenched hand. Peter kept on convulsing as more firebugs pierced through him. Everyone except Werner, Klaus and Nancy had fled into the computer room with the firebugs in hot pursuit.

"We've opened a portal to the dreamweave," Klaus yelled as he ducked from a firebug, "That bracelet must be the key." He then yelped as a firebug grazed a thigh.

Werner, who was cornered trying to deflect the firebugs with a metal tray, yelled out, "Nancy, we need to get that bracelet away from Peter to close the portal." He took a large swing and hit three firebugs into the next room, which was total pandemonium with over two-dozen firebugs terrorizing the staff.

The dreaming den was now filling with smoke as the firebugs ran into equipment, igniting then on contact. Nancy tried to pry the bracelet out of his hand, but Peter was in a death grip as more firebugs came through him. She was still trying to pry it loose when she moved back a step and screamed while still holding on.

Klaus had been busy unstringing and activating the fire

hose just outside the den when he heard Nancy's scream. His eyes opened wide when he saw what looked like a ribbon of fire that moved like a snake coming out of Peter's chest. He turned around and frantically turned the water valve on. Another scream had him turn again, this time grabbing the fire nozzle and rushing into the den.

Werner was now protecting Nancy as he swatted away the firebugs coming near or the new ones popping out of Peter. He really didn't know how Peter could still be alive. He was a mess of charred holes and he just kept shuddering. Suddenly, a ribbon of fire came out of Peter's chest and acted like the end of a whip. He swatted with the tray at it as Nancy screamed. The fire whip didn't seem to like that and fought back by hitting the metal tray. The fire whip then stopped, and almost like it had eyes, the tip turned and looked at the bracelet. The fire whip was motionless for a second and then it attacked like a cobra. Nancy's primal scream was still in the air when Klaus ran into the den with the fire hose. He stopped and stared as the fire whip curled around the part of the bracelet that Nancy did not have her fingers on and started pulling. A three-way struggle for the bracelet ensued with Peter's death grip locked around it and with Nancy's two hands trying to pry it out of his hand. The fire whip now looped around a portion of the bracelet and pulled with unimaginable strength.

"Oh no you don't, you bastard!" she yelled and really started to wrench on the bracelet. The fire whip, sensing the added strength, moved around the bracelet and now came into contact with Nancy's fingers. A scream of agony erupted from Nancy as she refused to let go, even as she watched her own fingers burn. Klaus snapped out of it and turned the fire nozzle on and pointed it toward the bracelet. The first stream of water just evaporated into steam as it hit Nancy and the fire whip. Within seconds Nancy began to sigh in relief. It was working. The fire whip still had a grip but no longer burnt.

Klaus looked up to Werner who was still busy swatting the firebugs. They caught each other's eyes and Werner yelled out, "That thing is not going to let go, is it Nancy?"

Nancy had both hands barely hanging on, "It's slipping. I don't have enough of a grip."

Werner ran to the door of the den, took a fleeting glance at the mayhem still going on in the next room and tried to slam the door shut only to be stopped by the fire hose.

"Damn it! Klaus we need to shut this door now," Werner looked at him.

Klaus who was busy spraying onto the bracelet looked over to him, "But -"

Werner cut him off, "Now Klaus! Trust me."

Nancy looked over to the two and nodded. Klaus didn't even take time to shut the hose off. He just threw the open end into the main room. Werner slammed the door. Nancy immediately began howling in pain as the fire whip renewed its attack.

"Everyone close your eyes and hold your breath!" Werner yelled. He smashed a small glass panel beside the door and pushed a large button. Immediately, from the six ceiling spraying jets, a fire suppression gas screamed out and filled the room. The firebugs, trapped in the dreaming den, were snuffed out and fell to the floor. The fire whip was also put out instantaneously. Within ten seconds, all fires were out and Nancy was still wrenching against Peter's grip. A fast acting exhaust system sucked out and replaced the fouled air.

Klaus was now helping Nancy uncurl Peter's last two fingers when three new firebugs came through.

"Not again!" Klaus yelled as a new tip of a fire whip came up through Peter's still shuddering body.

Tony and Manuel were now permanently on the floor of the balcony as the shockwaves were consistently hitting *Here*. Darkness surrounded what was left, as the multitude clambered over each other trying to escape.

"End time comes to *Here*," the Being said floating still beside the two.

Tony just closed his eyes and thought to himself, "Good try my friend, good try."

The positive dreamhub was on fire. Over eighty percent of the occupants were still there, trying to flee in one direction only to run into another fleeing mass. Thousands of more firebugs and other nightmarish atrocities materialized from the black cloud mass of the neg-hub to try to finish it off.

In the real world, hundreds of towns and cities were now in states of panic as their neighborhoods ignited throughout the night. Emergency crews could not cope and anarchy began to rear its ugly head.

Werner was swatting the new swarm of firebugs coming out of Peter as both Nancy and Klaus worked on the bracelet. Klaus struggled as four fire whips were now in this assault. Klaus was trying his best to protect Nancy as she almost started clawing at Peter's fingers.

"He won't give it up!" she half screamed in frustration and was lanced by a fifth fire whip that just appeared.

"Werner!" Klaus yelled. He was in more pain than he had ever felt before. "Hit that button again." There was no reply from Werner behind them, only the sound of firebugs buzzing.

"Werner!" Klaus screamed as another three fire whips appeared. Klaus glanced at his hands that resembled partially cooked meat. It became too much and Klaus looked upward with his eyes closed and screamed in agony. He then moved toward his right instinctively as he felt a very fast motion and wind go past his left side. The sound of metal on metal hit his eardrum and then Nancy yelled, "Noooooo!"

Both Nancy and Klaus fell to the floor. Werner stood over them with a large bloodied fire ax. Peter's arm was in Klaus's mangled hands. Nancy had crumpled to the floor.

Nancy sat up in shock as the sounds of sobbing,

scuffling bodies and electrical crackling filled both rooms. She got up, placing her right hand on the plastic perimeter for support and looked down at Peter.

Peter just lay there finally still with charred holes through his lifeless body. Blood oozed out of his recently severed left stump. All the fire whips and firebugs had just vanished in both rooms.

"I'm so sorry Nancy," Werner said sincerely. "The fire system was only good for one charge. There was no other choice."

Nancy stifled a small scream and raised her left hand to wipe away some tears. She had the bracelet in her grip. The death of Peter, her love, was forgotten now for an instant as she gazed upon the brilliant bracelet of gold.

EPILOGUE

Ultimately, the effects of Fritz's negative dreamhub, of which the world was still oblivious to, were overwhelming in their immensity. Over two million had perished with ten times that number left homeless because of the property destruction. Insurance estimates were staggering: over a trillion dollars and climbing rapidly. One major insurance company had already registered for Chapter 11 - Bankruptcy.

Religious leaders around the globe proclaimed that the wrath of the almighty was upon the sinful earth. Governments struggled to respond to relief efforts as pockets of anarchy still existed in razed villages and small cities.

The markets acted predictably, plunging in the frantic environment, only to rebound better than ever because of speculation of a reconstruction boom for the next few years.

That fateful night, when the bracelet talisman

materialized into this world, at that instant, both artificial dreamhubs went out like two supernovas. Millions of dreamlines, each on their own path, shot out away from the hubs. Some creating natural dreamhubs, some back on their original paths.

The positive shockwave created by the collapsing hubs reached *Here* at the velocity of light speed. Untold number of stranded souls including Tony and Manuel, who had died throughout the sixty years of Fritz's experiments, were finally released from *Here*, off to parts unknown. *Here* returned to its original state, with a new brilliant gold bracelet adorning the Being's wrist.

A helicopter landed in the very early morning. Four CTU agents rapidly exited and secured the landing pad of the compound in Costa Rica. Ted, the new CEO of Zicon, stepped out brandishing an automatic pistol in his hand. With two agents at his side, they approached the command post. Looking through the windows they knew why their calls had been unanswered. They quickly went to the main lab. The two agents silently entered while Ted waited outside. Within a few seconds, one agent came out and waved him in. Inside on a couch, Fritz was fully passed out and snoring loudly. A bottle of expensive single malt scotch, which stood on a side table, was mostly empty. Ted took a look at the old man still wearing his tattered SS tunic. He raised his pistol, but his finger could not pull the trigger.

"He doesn't deserve this," he said, "Rig it," he directed the agents. Plastic explosives came out of black satchels and the agents started placing the charges and timers in the lab and other buildings of the compound.

Ted walked over to the main control panel. So much destruction and death from this, he thought.

Ten minutes later the agent reported, "All set sir. Thirty minutes and counting."

"I'll meet you at the copter," Ted said without looking at the agent. The agent looked from Ted to Fritz and turned around and left. Ted took a couple of minutes setting some controls and then pressed the activate button. He left the lab without looking at Fritz and climbed into the helicopter.

High above, still in orbit, the satellite received its new commands and commenced broadcasting for the last time image streams of men burning on crosses to a very remote part of Costa Rica. Fritz's nightmare began.

Fritz had been in a deep alcohol induced slumber, dreaming of having a leisurely early evening dinner with Adolf and Eva. The air was crisp on the outside patio of The Berchtesgaden, Adolf's mountain bastion. Actual memories were mixed in with his dream of that night long ago. The conversation was light until Eva excused herself from the table. Adolf leaned in and asked Fritz about his upcoming experiments. Fritz got excited and sitting on the edge of his chair began describing the preparations and step of procedures soon to be taken. Adolf sat mesmerized, listening to Fritz with a slight smile on his face. Fritz carried on until he noticed that Adolf had not moved. It was like he was frozen in time. Fritz looked up into the sky to see a flock of ravens hanging still in the air.

Fritz stood up, his chair moving back scratching across the patio. He turned toward the house and saw Eva in a frozen mid-walk coming back on to the patio. He turned back toward Adolf only to find himself now standing on hard packed ground. He was back at Janowska, the first concentration camp he had experimented at.

A still scene was also in front of him. The camp was exactly as he had remembered: the barbed fencing, guard towers and rows and rows of prisoner barracks. What was unsettling was the two very long rows of shabbily dressed individuals stretched out in front of Fritz like a gauntlet. The rows faced each other about four feet apart, their heads turned looking at Fritz with grim expressions. The rows extended from Fritz toward the horizon. Suddenly, hundreds of voices came alive.

Fritz watched in growing apprehension as the two rows shouted at him in multiple languages, not moving, only shouting the same phrase, "You are part of an experiment. Do not struggle." The very words he had used so many times before. That is when he clued in and recognized the first few men. They had been his first subjects.

Immediately Fritz backed up only to hit an invisible wall. He tried both right and left with the same result. He was trapped and there was only one way to go. He stood there hearing the taunts, not fearful of dying but fearful of the pain before dying. Straightening his posture and adjusting his SS Jacket, Fritz began walking toward the beginning of the two rows. Within three feet of the first two men, they stopped their chant and began speaking to Fritz.

"My name is Joseph Loewy. I had two children," said one.

"Mein name ist Leon Meyer," said the other in German.

They both suddenly began to show burns and disfigurement from what Fritz had done to them. Within arms-length they quickly lunged at Fritz to touch him. Searing pain erupted from his sides where their fingertips had made contact. Each touch felt like the flame of an acetylene torch.

Fritz twisted away toward the next pair only to hear them start up also, "My name is…" He looked back to see the first two transform to healthy vibrant men in clean clothing. They both turned and began to follow Fritz. More searing pain enveloped Fritz as more fingers lanced at his body, and again he twisted away stumbling toward the third pair. And so it went for at least an hour. Fritz's mind felt like jelly with the constant pain and images of his tormentors. The rows were arms-length. The huge crowd behind just continued following him with smiles on their faces as they watched Fritz's march of death. Fritz was in tatters by now. His skin and clothing burnt with charred circular welts. Even parts of his hair had gone up in flames when it had been touched.

Despair finally took a hold of Fritz as he looked down the still long rows. Did I really do this many experiments? he thought as he continued on. The pain was a constant part of him when finally he actually saw a light at the end of the rows. He still had about ten pairs to go, but he could see the outline of flickering light.

"My name is Manuel," said the last man in the row. "This is your destiny." He then waved his hand backwards. Fritz, who was almost a crisp of a man by now looked up to a small line of large crosses. Each cross had one of his former associates tied to it like a crucifixion. Each burned in agony from an engulfing flame surrounding them, but was still alive. Fritz closed his eyes and lowered his head not in a silent prayer but in sheer frustration. Why can't I just die? he thought.

"You must live through each of our torment," Manuel said looking back behind Fritz to the mass of followers, "then you may pass through."

Fritz started to say something when he opened his eyes. His view was distorted by yellow flame flowing up his body as he looked down from his perch on the cross at the smiling mass below. The pain was so intense that it began to be a friend to Fritz, something to concentrate on.

He noticed that every once in a while, one from the crowd would simply disappear. He concluded that, when he relived one's pain, that one would leave while he went on to the next. The screams of his assistants beside him broke his will not to feel and he began wailing with them. Time escaped him as he watched the mass dwindle, reliving each of his experiments.

Now down to the last two, Manuel spoke again. "Finally our souls have been released. May yours find its own way." Manuel then vanished. And finally, the last of the tormented, the girl from Costa Rica also winked out.

"Welcome to *Here*," said the beautiful Being. Fritz looked about and was mesmerized by the grandeur and vibrant colors surrounding him.

"Where am I?" he asked looking out from a large balcony over the endless terrain.

"This is *Here*," the Being waved her arm toward the expanse and then noticed that her new bracelet had tarnished slightly.

"Indeed it is. Indeed," Fritz smiled.

"You are not supposed to be here," said the tall very strange looking entity cloaked in an ever-changing garment.

Peter tried to take in everything within his sight. The room was completely dark except for this entity. No sense of the room's size could be measured. The entity's flowing garments all seemed to meld into each other; biblical, twentieth century, medieval, all lasting just seconds.

"Where am I?" Peter said not knowing if he really wanted to know.

"This is *Before*."

"Oh shit," Peter said.

**Watch out for Peter Sutherland's
next exciting journey
coming soon.**

www.erikgraham.net

Author Photo by Michael Graham

Erik Graham is an Internet entrepreneur with various ventures on the go. Dreamweave is his first novel, but not his last. He presently lives in beautiful Vancouver, British Columbia, Canada where you can find him writing on a beach somewhere or on Joe Fortes patio.

www.erikgraham.net